A FOREVER DAD

SEALS IN PARADISE - HOLIDAY EDITION / A HOPE CITY CROSSOVER NOVEL

MARYANN JORDAN

D1603269

ISBN ebook: 978-1-947214-78-1

ISBN: print: 978-1-947214-79-8

❀ Created with Vellum

"Never too early for a beer!"

Ben "Pops" Popovich grinned as he stood with the tight-knit group of men he called brothers as well as friends and accepted the icy can from Gage. The California sun was not high in the sky but on the cloudless day the heat was already penetrating, causing a mirage of waves rising from the parking lot asphalt. "Gator, truer words were never spoken." He held the can to his lips and let the cold brew slide down his throat, trying not to think that this was the last time he'd probably bend an elbow with these men all at the same time. Times were changing, and it was all he could do to focus on the needs of the day, not what lay ahead.

"Here's to Pops and new fuckin' adventures," Cole shouted, holding up his beer before drinking, joining with the others.

Brian leaned against Ben's new SUV and shook his head. "Hard to imagine you without your bike."

Ben looked over at Brian, known as Heartbreaker to the group, a moniker which now seemed wrong considering he was now shackled to the beautiful Alicia... and from one look at Brian, the man was damn happy about it.

"Not gonna get his grannie on the back of his bike," Joker grinned.

"That's for damn sure. Hell, you've installed April on the back of yours, but all I've got is my grandmother," he laughed. Ignoring the reminder of why he was leaving his SEAL team with an honorable discharge after fifteen years in the service, he directed his smile toward Joker, another friend whose single status had bitten the dust.

"Pops, what I can't get over is how you managed to get all your worldly possessions into the back of this SUV with room to spare," Chris said, peering into the back. "Damn, man, don't you have more shit somewhere?"

Finishing his beer, he leveled his gaze onto Zig and shrugged as though he hadn't a care in the world. "Fuck, what's the use of spending my money on shit that I don't use 'cause we were always somewhere fuckin' else?" The others nodded in varying degrees of agreement, but he couldn't help but glance into the back of the SUV and see the boxes and bags that contained the entirety of his possessions. After years of living in barracks or renting small, furnished efficiency apartments that came with dishes and pots, he barely owned more than his clothes, linens, some books, a laptop, and a few mementos.

He'd been in the service since he was eighteen, earning an associate degree along the way before becoming a SEAL. Creating a *home* had never been on his list of things to do, focus on his career taking precedence over everything else. After all, he could never recreate what had been *home* with his grandparents. Now, at thirty-three, with all his possessions packed into the back of the vehicle he'd just bought after trading in his motorcycle, he scrubbed his hand over his face, ready to go back to what had been *home*, praying it wouldn't be so different from what he remembered.

"How long do you figure it'll take you to get to Hope City?" Gage asked.

"Hell, from California to the east coast? It's about forty hours or so. Figure I'll break it up into four days. I could make it in three, but then I'd get there late and don't want to bother my grandmother after she's gone to bed. If I arrive the next day, it'll be better."

"You okay with everything?" Cole asked, his smile still firmly in place but his gaze penetrating.

The others' mirth slowed as they waited for his answer, knowing the atmosphere was different from the good luck party they'd thrown the other night at their team leader Bear's house, where alcohol had flowed as much as the glory stories they told and embellished.

He nodded slowly, the truth of what he was about to say moving through him painfully. "Been a helluva career, guys. Couldn't have asked for a better team to go out with. But family duty calls, and it's time for that to take precedence over Uncle Sam's needs. Plus, three fuckin' knee repairs in the past years. Even if it wasn't for my grandmother getting sick, this body isn't what it used to be. There are younger men—although not *better* men—ready to take over." That statement brought a round of 'hear, hears', and he laughed along with them.

Crumpling his beer can, he tossed it expertly into the trash bin in the parking lot and looked around at the best men he'd ever known. Training, missions, no sleep on cold nights, and running on adrenaline during blistering hot days. Vacations with palm trees and women looking to score a SEAL in between missions hanging out of helicopters over Godforsaken countries where if it hadn't been for each other, they'd have never made it home.

He dragged in a deep breath before letting it out slowly. "Goodbyes suck ass, but they've got to be said."

One by one, his friends walked over, man-hugs and hearty back-slaps ensuing. Feeling the tightness in his throat, he offered a final chin lift and climbed into the driver's seat. Starting the engine, he rolled the window down and called out, "If you're ever on the east coast, look me up. Hope City… as good as the name implies."

With that, he tossed his hand up with a two-fingered salute and pulled out of the parking lot of the semi-crappy apartment building he'd called home between missions for the past two years. Ignoring the brick and crumbling stucco, he looked into the rearview mirror and said another silent goodbye to the members of his SEAL team. When they were no longer in sight, he sucked in another deep, cleansing breath and stared forward. Long road ahead. But at the end was the woman who'd raised him, nurtured him, made it her mission to ensure he became the man he was. And now, she needed him.

"On my way home to Babciu." With that thought, he flipped on the radio and settled in for the long drive.

2

Four days later, Ben drove down the familiar, tree-lined street, observing only a few changes and upgrades to the houses along the way. It had been over two years since he'd last visited his grandmother. Much of Hope City's housing was made of brick townhomes built over a hundred and fifty years ago for the dockworkers and immigrants that flooded the city in the 1800s. In the area closest to the downtown docks, they were packed tightly together, block after block, neighborhoods filled with square streets and narrow homes with no back-yards other than tiny, concrete courtyards. As he drove further away from the downtown area, the townhomes were a bit larger and most included backyards with grass and trees, appearing less industrial.

His grandmother's house was on such a street, and seeing the neighborhood through adult eyes, he could see how fortunate he'd been. His grandparents had taken an end unit, bought the townhouse next to it, and renovated the two to make one large home with a full backyard. Considering there was a park across the street, he'd had plenty of places to play.

He had spent the long drive from California listening to audiobooks, music, podcasts... anything to keep from facing what he might find when he arrived in Hope City. His grandmother had called the previous month after a mild stroke, asking for recommendations about getting the house ready to sell so that she could move into an independent living facility. *Fuck that!* His grandfather had been a contractor and had always handled the renovations and repairs, teaching Ben what he knew. The idea of his grandmother being taken advantage of by someone unknown... *not gonna happen.* And he hated the idea of her moving.

Plus, with the problems he had with his knee, a joint that now was as good an indicator of impending bad weather as the best meteorologist, it was time to separate from the military.

Coming to the intersection, he looked out the windshield as the house came into view. Red brick with a dark green front door and matching shutters on the windows. Two stories with a third-floor bonus room and deck. His gaze dropped to the side and the chainlink fence around the neatly trimmed backyard. The familiarity of the view had memories rushing through his mind, and a smile slid over his face as his heart warmed.

Pulling to a stop just outside the front door near the corner, he parked and climbed out of the SUV. Stretching his arms over his head, he twisted back and forth, working out the kinks from the trip. Hurrying up the front steps, he slid his key into the keyhole, unsure if his grandmother was resting. Opening the front door, he was hit with the familiar scent of her kolachzi cookies and the sound of music coming from the kitchen.

"Babciu?" The Polish word for grandmother was the only word from the old world that had been passed down through the family, so familiar to him since that's what she'd called her grandmother.

"Benjamin! Is that you?" came the cry from the back.

A wide grin spread over his face as he hurried through the living room, through the dining room, and into the huge kitchen where his grandmother was walking toward him, her cane in her hand but not leaned upon. Her soft, white hair, cut just above her shoulders, floated about her face. Her blue eyes were bright and her smile wide, deepening the creases emanating from her eyes. A red apron was tied about her waist, the bib protecting her bright yellow blouse and tan pants. She halted her progress as he moved past the counter and wrapped his arms around her, enveloping her into his embrace as the scent of her soft perfume wafted past. Her arms encircled his waist, and she patted his back, just like when he was much younger.

"I didn't know when to expect you." She leaned back to hold his gaze, her eyes searching over his face before narrowing. "Did you drive straight through from California?"

"Well, I stopped for food and sleep," he laughed. His gaze took her in, carefully cataloging the changes since he last saw her. She was a little thinner, and her smile was slightly crooked, making him wonder if it was due to the stroke.

"Let's sit down." He wanted her off her feet, but she shook her head.

"I've got one more batch of cookies in the oven—"

"I'll get them when your timer goes off. Come on, sit with me." He hovered as she turned and walked toward the table.

When his grandfather renovated the two townhouses into one, he kept the front separated, creating a formal living room, dining room, and powder room on one side, and on the other side, a family den and sitting room. But in the back of the house, he combined the two kitchen spaces, making one huge kitchen with modern appliances, lots of counters, and a family table for everyday eating. A full bathroom and laundry were just off from the kitchen. A sliding glass door opened to the backyard, allowing sunlight to pour into the space. It was Ben's favorite room in the house, and even now, over twenty years later, he reveled in the comfort.

Once she was settled, he grabbed the platter of cooled cookies and placed them on the table. He noted a cup of tea steeping on the counter and placed that in front of his grandmother as well. Grabbing a glass of milk from the refrigerator, he sat next to her, eagerly reaching for the first kolachzi he'd had in a couple of years. Biting into the buttery-sweet cookie, he groaned as the strawberry jam hit his taste buds.

"Oh, Babciu, this is amazing. I've missed your cooking."

She smiled, patting his hand before taking a cookie herself, closing her eyes as she chewed. "Your grandfather always said kolachzi was one of my best recipes. It belonged to my babcia, you know."

He nodded while stuffing another cookie into his mouth. His great-grandfather had immigrated to the United States from Poland as a young man, bringing his young bride. They settled into the Polish neighborhoods of Hope City. Anna was their youngest child, and she married Ben's grandfather, a man whose grandparents had immigrated from Poland as well.

Swallowing his bite, he washed it down with cold milk before leaning back in his chair and heaving a satisfied sigh. "Grandpa was right, but then I've never had anything you cooked that wasn't amazing."

"Benjamin, I never expected you to visit when I called you, but you know my heart is singing with you being here. So, tell me, how long are you here for? Do I dare hope you can stay a week? If so, I promise to cook all my specialties to tempt you!"

He scrubbed his hand over his short hair, glad for the reprieve when the buzzer for the oven timer sounded. Jumping to his feet, he walked over and gloved his hand with her large oven mitt before opening the door. Taking the opportunity to stall for a moment, he set the last tray of cookies onto the stovetop. With her spatula, he gently slid them onto the cooling rack. Taking the tray to the sink, he looked out the window framed with sunny curtains in a checked pattern of yellow, green, and blue.

He remembered her telling him that the house

directly behind hers had been empty for a while but now the grass was trimmed, and several toys were in the yard. Curtains hung on their kitchen window as well. Turning his back to the window, he glanced around to see what else he could do to busy himself, but her words cut through his thoughts.

"You're stalling, Benjamin."

He looked over at her, finding her peering at him through her glasses, her sharp eyes on his face. Sighing, he nodded and walked back to the table, slumping into the chair. "What would you say if I told you that I'm not going back in a week?"

She startled slightly and shook her head. "Oh, no, Benjamin. You're not going to give up everything to stay here with me! I'm fine. The stroke was not serious, and I don't need you to sacrifice your career for me. You help me find a qualified contractor, and then I can get this place ready to sell."

He held her gaze then grinned sheepishly. "You never did let me get away with anything, did you?"

"Bah," she chuckled, waving her hand. "What's on your mind? What are you not telling me?" Leaning back, she added, "You'll make me worry if I have to guess."

"You missed your calling. You should have been an interrogator. You could make the most hardened terrorist want to spill their guts."

Her mirth now poured forth as she laughed, her eyes twinkling. Finished stalling, he held her hand, noting the strength in her fingers. "It was time." She said nothing, her patience allowing his story to come as it would.

"Your phone call didn't start the change in my life. I

was already having to make some difficult decisions. Fifteen years in the service... thirteen of those as a SEAL. I was lucky. I got to work with the best people doing a job I loved. But change comes to us all."

"Your injuries." Her plainly stated comment was soft and full of understanding.

"Yeah." He sighed his acknowledgment. "The first knee injury involved physical therapy, but I was anxious to get back to my team, so I jumped in to do whatever I had to do to get cleared. The second injury of the same knee included surgery, followed by PT and rehab. And a stern warning about the joint being weakened."

"As we get older, our bodies don't heal as quickly as we would like, even at your young age."

Her words pricked his thick skin. Thirty-three wasn't old, and he was luckier than many. But eventually, his luck ran out. A third serious injury involved more surgery, more PT, more rehab.

"Yeah. The next injury caused me the most problem with my superiors." He had been called into the commander's office and told that if he couldn't keep up, he'd be sidelined on upcoming missions. He'd nodded his understanding but walked out pissed at the world. Waking up each morning with a stiff and aching knee despite his determination only made it worse. Then came his grandmother's call.

She stiffened her back and huffed. "They can't kick you out! You're too valuable—"

"Whoa, tiger," he laughed, rubbing his hand over hers. "No one kicked me out. But I knew I needed to make some decisions. Your call came at the perfect time.

You needed some help... I needed to make a career change."

"What are you saying, Benjamin? Speak plainly."

His grandmother never beat around the bush, always speaking what was on her mind and desiring the same from those around her. It sure as hell made it easier to not have to guess what was on her mind. "Okay, here it is. I'm not going back." He heard her sharp intake of breath and kept going. "I have officially retired from military service. I've come back to Hope City to help you fix this house, help you find a place to live if you want, and make a new start for myself."

"Well," she said, leaning back in her chair.

Her gaze stayed pinned on him, and he fought the urge to squirm under her perusal. "So, uh... what do you think?"

She chuckled, squeezing his fingers. "I think I'm pleased to have you back home." She rose from her chair, and with her cane, made her way to the sink before looking over her shoulder. "But I don't want you to hover. I am still independent, although having you back home is a dream come true that I never thought would happen. Now, bring the glasses over. We have dishes to wash."

Lying in bed that night, Ben stretched out on the comfortable mattress. Just as his grandfather had reworked the downstairs space, the same had been accomplished upstairs. The two original townhouses each had three small bedrooms upstairs with one bathroom accessible from the hall. He had opened the six bedrooms and created four large bedrooms, modernized the bathrooms, and gave the main bedroom its own large bathroom.

Looking around, Ben was once again glad that his grandmother had not clung to the idea that he would always remain a child. The bedroom of his youth had been redecorated with a queen-sized bed and dark blue sheets with a gray and blue comforter. The sports posters that had graced the walls when he was a teenager had been replaced with several skyline pictures of Hope City, and a few framed photographs of the family perched on top of the wooden chest of drawers that had remained the same. The desk near the window where he used to complete his homework had been replaced by a thick-cushioned chair and ottoman with a reading lamp and end table next to them.

He couldn't remember how long he'd been in the service when he came home to discover the room had been redecorated from boy-style to man-appropriate, but it had been appreciated then as now. His grandmother was a practical as well as astute woman.

He rolled to the side and looked at the framed photograph of him and his parents in front of the Christmas tree when he was ten years old. It was the last picture he had of them. When they were killed soon after, his father's parents swooped in. He'd spent many hours with them as a younger child, so their home was as familiar to him as his own. Their love and devotion helped a sad and angry young boy to mature and grow into the kind of man his parents would have wanted him to be. His grandparents had given so much to be surrogate parents that for him to spend time helping his grandmother now would be easy.

He'd spent the rest of the afternoon and evening walking around the house, taking a look at what needed to be done. The structure was sound, and it appeared that only cosmetic changes would need to be made for it to fetch a high price in a robust market. Rooms needed a fresh coat of paint. Wooden floors needed to be polished and buffed. He detected a few cracks in some of the old windows and decided that it was time for them to be replaced.

The plumbing was sound as was the wiring, and while his grandfather had updated the bathrooms and kitchen years ago, they could use another facelift. The yard was in good shape, but the deck was old and small, and the image of a brick patio large enough for a built-in grill had taken shape in Ben's mind. It would take time and money, both of which he had.

On his back, he stared at the ceiling and smiled. His grandmother, while showing signs of the slight stroke, had been in surprisingly good health. With him here, she'd be able to stay in her beloved home longer while he completed the renovations. *Would she still want to sell?* If so, he had no idea what he'd do with his life.

Rolling over, he thought of the next day. He'd go over the entire house in-depth, figuring out what needed to be completed, and make a schedule for the work. Finally, with tomorrow's plans in place, he closed his eyes, welcoming sleep.

3

"Mom!"

Violet Mayfield sighed. The shout from her daughter Lily was not one of fear or need… it was the sound of *want*. She might love the job of being a mom, but hearing it shouted from one end of the house to another constantly could be a bit tiring. And it all had to be carried on her shoulders.

She walked into the small living room and spied her six-year-old son, Charlie, jumping toward Lily, who was holding the TV remote over his head. Lily, normally an adorable, nine-year-old, wonderful sister, was not above using her slight height advantage to keep something away from Charlie. Violet knew that as soon as Charlie hit a growth spurt in a couple of years he would surpass Lily in height, taking after their father. Then, her ever-resourceful daughter would have to find a new way to stay ahead of her brother.

Lifting a brow, she stepped further into the room and planted her hands on her hips. "Is there a reason why you two are shouting like banshees over the remote? And since there's homework to do, I would advise you to consider your answer carefully."

Both children's mouths had opened, ready to tell their side of the story, when they snapped shut. Eyes wide, they glanced between each other and her. Wisely, Lily clicked the TV off and placed the remote on the coffee table.

"I'm done," Charlie pronounced, eyeing the remote longingly.

"I'm almost done," Lily said. "But it's not fair. I have more to do than he does. Fourth grade is a lot harder than first grade."

"That might be, but you also get more perks to go along with the responsibility of being older."

She hid her smile as she watched her daughter noodle through that concept, letting out a small sigh of relief when her daughter nodded her agreement.

"Okay, Charlie," Lily conceded. "I've got at least fifteen more minutes of homework and then we can play."

Charlie nodded, then looked up toward Violet. "While she finishes, can I show you what I did?"

"Of course. Let's go into the kitchen so we can leave your sister alone while she works." Charlie grabbed his papers from the coffee table and darted toward the kitchen, barely slowing down enough for her to ruffle her fingers through his hair. Turning toward Lily, she bent and kissed the top of her daughter's head, mumbling, "Thank you, sweetie."

She and Charlie sat at the kitchen table, and she

offered her full attention as he reviewed his spelling and math homework. By the time they'd finished, Lily had joined them, and Violet had finished making dinner: hot dogs, macaroni and cheese, and sweet peas. It wasn't the best dinner a mom could provide but considering both kids were going through picky-eater phases, she was glad to find something they'd both eat.

Winter had just passed, but the spring weather in Hope City was ever-changing. Their backyard received the most direct sunlight, and she shooed the kids out to play in the fresh air after calling out to them to grab jackets.

Moving back to the sink, she washed dishes and allowed her mind to wander over her workday. Dropping her chin to her chest, she sighed. If only she had finished her college degree before getting married. It was harder now as a widow with two children to take classes part-time, but she was so close to graduating with a degree in management, she could almost taste it. And then she could afford to find a new job with a new boss… one that hopefully would consider her to be more than office decoration while staring at her chest all day.

Her title was bookkeeper for a small company, but when the owner died a year ago, his nephew took over. It was then that her fun job with a nice boss changed, and her days were now spent as barely more than a receptionist who answered the phone, took messages, and fetched coffee. *As well as avoid his constant invitations to dinner.* She had no interest in her boss, and the way his eyes dropped to her breasts every time he talked to her made her skin crawl.

She rinsed the dishes and put them into the rack to dry. There were other jobs available, but she'd worked for the company since pregnant with Lily and she'd built up sick days to take when needed for the kids. Her former boss has been so good during her bereavement leave when Matt died. She also had health insurance through them... a true bonus with young kids.

Moving to the back door, her gaze landed on the kids as they kicked a ball back and forth, shouting encouragement for each other. As she so often did, she stood at the doorway and watched, knowing if she looked into a mirror, she would see a sad smile... tinged with anger. Charlie had his father's dark brown hair and her blue eyes and one day would have his height. Lily took after her with black hair paired with dark blue eyes. And, like Violet, would probably be more petite.

"If only you could have seen them grow up, Matt." Her whispered words were soft, for no one's ears other than her own. And because he was gone, there was no answer. She'd been widowed for three years, and while the ache had diminished, for each milestone her children reached was the knowledge that she, alone, celebrated their achievements. Giving her head a little shake to dislodge the maudlin thoughts, she turned to pull clean towels from the dryer and fold them.

As the sun moved to a place in the sky that cast long shadows over the backyard, she walked to the door to call her children into the house. A man was standing on her backyard neighbor's small deck. She'd met Anna

Popovich when they moved in six months ago. The delightful older woman had proven to be a sweet neighbor, occasionally watching the children when their after-school care closed early. She had appreciated Anna's volunteering to babysit whenever Violet needed, but after Anna's slight stroke the month before, she didn't want to add to the woman's burden. The children loved visiting her, coming back with tales of sweet cookies and the third-floor balcony that Charlie swore allowed him to see to the ends of the earth.

Whereas Violet's end-unit townhome was only two stories and narrow, Anna's had a basement and a third-floor bonus room, technically making it four stories as well as being extra-wide with two townhomes put together. Her home was just enough for her little family of three but she wistfully knew that in a few years when the kids were older, a home Anna's size would be desirable. *Maybe, by then, I can afford something larger.*

The man standing on Anna's deck had hands on his hips, his gaze scanning the area. As though hearing her children's laughter, he looked toward her house and Violet blinked in surprise. Dark hair, dark scruff on his jaws, and with his sleeves pushed up, his arm muscles were on display. A little sigh escaped. *He's certainly handsome.*

As though he could hear her thoughts, he lifted his gaze from the backyard to the door where she was standing. She battled the automatic response to move out of his sight, continuing to stare. He turned away from her and walked to Mrs. Popovich's door. She wondered if he was a contractor since Anna had mentioned hoping to get work done. She watched the older woman open the back door and reach up to pat his cheek as the man stepped inside. *Her grandson!* Violet remembered that Anna mentioned her grandson was coming for a visit. *Good. Hopefully, he can help her get some work done while he's here.* She glanced down to see her children were quiet, their gazes riveted on the man who'd walked inside Anna's house. Opening her door, she called them in, laughing as they bounded into the small laundry room at the back of the house that led into the kitchen, both talking over each other about the man on Mrs. Popovich's deck.

"I've never seen that man!" Charlie said, pulling off his jacket. "I wonder who he was?"

"Mrs. Popovich told me she was going to have her grandson visit." Lily hung up her coat, hanging it on a peg as well. Turning her dark eyes toward her mom, she asked, "Do you think that's who it was?"

Thinking about the loving gesture Mrs. Popovich offered the man, she nodded. "I think that probably was her grandson."

Charlie's face fell. "I thought maybe her grandson would be my age. Somebody I could play with."

"That's dumb, Charlie. Mrs. Popovich is old. She can't have a grandson our age!"

"Mom, she called me dumb!"

"I did not!"

"Charlie! Lily!" Violet clapped her hands, gaining their attention. "Lily, even though you didn't call your brother dumb, it wasn't nice to put down what he said. And Charlie, I know you don't realize this, but Mrs.

Popovich is about the same age as my grandmother, so her grandson is probably closer to my age." She watched as Charlie's brow crinkled in thought before smiling. Bending, she placed a kiss on each of their heads. "Wash your hands, and we can have some ice cream and a little TV time before you get ready for bed."

With whoops of joy, her children ran off toward the downstairs powder room. Glancing back toward Mrs. Popovich's house, she smiled. She'd been worried about the older woman who valued her independence. She tried to remember what Mrs. Popovich had said about her grandson... *he was in the military... her pride and joy... a good man. Well, he's certainly good-looking from a distance, that's for sure.*

Dipping the ice cream into three bowls, the thought of Mrs. Popovich moving caused a sigh to slip out. It was so nice to let Charlie and Lily out into the yard without having to worry about who might be in the yard behind them. Of course, being on an end unit, she had to worry about people on the side street but had constantly warned the kids to not play near the side fence. Pushing thoughts of her neighbor's grandson out of her mind, she carried a tray with ice cream into the living room, indulging her children before bedtime.

Benjamin locked the back door after having checked the deck measurements and scoping out an area for a patio with a built-in grill. He had noticed two children playing in the yard behind his grandmother's, but by the time they noticed him, he was almost finished with his initial estimate of the deck area. He'd never spent a lot of time around kids until recently. His SEAL team had adopted the widow and son of another teammate who had been killed in action. He'd enjoyed the time spent with Jeremy, as did all the team. Others on the base were married with kids, but he usually hung out with the singles.

It looked like the backyard neighbor kids were younger than Jeremy. *Hope that's not going to be a problem when I start working.* The idea of having to be the mean guy when making sure the kids weren't coming over when he was using tools or trying to climb on piles of wood didn't sit well with him. *Hopefully, their parents will make sure they stay on their side of the fence.*

His grandmother was standing at the kitchen counter, a cup of tea and a beer sitting on a tray. "I usually have my evening snack in the kitchen, but with you here, we can have it in the family room."

Dutifully carrying the tray, he followed her into the den, making sure her teacup was set on the end table next to her chair. He snagged his beer and sank into the deep cushions of the overstuffed sofa. Most of the rooms in the house had stayed the same since the time his grandfather had been living. The den held the comfortable sofa, the recliner his grandfather loved, and the high-backed chair his grandmother loved to sit in. Family photographs graced the walls and a bookcase held more framed pictures as well as an assortment of hardbacks and paperbacks, lovingly read over the years.

A refurbished stereo cabinet was against the far wall,

its ability to play vinyl records long gone but instead was used as the TV stand. She did have a wide, flat-screen TV thanks to Ben, who'd given her the present last Christmas. At first, she claimed to not need it but now was profusive in her appreciation of being able to see the television shows without straining her eyes.

"Did you have a chance to meet the Mayfields?"

He swallowed his first swig of beer, his gaze moving over to his grandmother. "I'm sorry? The Mayfields?"

"The family that lives behind us. I saw the children in the yard and thought perhaps you met them."

Shaking his head, he watched as she sipped her tea then set it back on the end table and placed her hands in her lap.

"I'm sure you'll have a chance to meet them now that you're going to be here."

"I don't want to encourage two children to be in the yard when I'm going to be working. They could get hurt on tools or wood or... whatever."

"I assure you they're very intelligent children," she insisted. "They wouldn't get in your way. Their mother is a lovely woman."

His beer threatened to go down wrong at her comment, the image of the woman standing in the doorway looking over at him hitting his mind. Her face had been indiscernible, obscured by the evening shadows. All he could truly see was that she was wearing pants and a dark top, hardly the sight to make a man sit up and take notice. Clearing his throat, he nodded. "I'm sure she is."

"They moved less than a year ago after that unfortunate incident with the man who owned the house before them."

"Unfortunate incident?" His brows lowered as he sat up straighter.

She sipped her tea and nodded. "Yes! It was quite the stir in the neighborhood at the time. Of course, I didn't know anything about the man until I looked out one morning and saw quite a few police cars around. I went out on the back deck—"

"Jesus, Babciu! You went outside when you saw a bunch of police?"

"Well, I didn't think I could be safer than when there were multiple policemen around! Anyway, are you going to let me tell my story?"

Huffing, he leaned back against the cushions, waiting to see what she was going to say next. She smiled and took another sip of tea, seeming to enjoy drawing out her tale.

"I'm afraid I didn't find out anything until it hit the news that evening. The man living behind me was a very unassuming-looking man who worked at one of the branches of the Hope City National Bank. Occasionally, we said hello if we happened to be out at the same time, and if there was snow, he would often move my trash cans to the street and back. I believe he lived alone, and he was so quiet, most of the time I never knew when he was there or not. I always thought it was strange that he had curtains over his kitchen window that stayed closed all the time. Most people like having sunshine in their kitchen—"

"The police?" he prodded, hiding his smile at her wandering tales.

"I'm getting to it. There was a robbery, and he was held at gunpoint along with several others in the bank. But I suppose, as the investigation took place, this man became a suspect as being in cahoots with the robber."

"Cahoots? Who uses the word cahoots anymore?"

Narrowing her gaze, she huffed. "Obviously, I do. Now hush, Benjamin!"

He grinned, nodding his acquiescence.

A smile slipped across her face as well, and she leaned forward, patting his knee. "The neighbor was arrested as well. And the house sat empty until the Mayfields moved there. So sweet, they are. It's nice to have good neighbors again."

Ben shook his head as he leaned forward, his forearms resting on his knees. "What a crazy story! How long was the house empty before the new family moved in?"

"For months... maybe almost a year, now that I think about it. I suppose, with all the notoriety, it was a little hard to sell. But one day, I looked over and there were children in the yard. I never wanted to frighten them, so I didn't mention the unfortunate incident. And I must say they are sweet neighbors." She took another sip of tea and then startled. "Oh, Ben... you mustn't mention it either. We don't want the children to be scared."

Ben hid his chuckle at her description of the *unfortunate incident* and shook his head. "I'm sure I won't be meeting the neighbors, at least no more than to say hello." *Plus, once this house is fixed up and sold, I'll have no choice but to move on.* A groan slipped out, knowing he had no idea where or to what he'd be moving on to.

Standing, he took his empty beer bottle and her teacup into the kitchen. Returning to the den, he assisted her into the sitting room where her makeshift bedroom had been set up so she did not have to traverse the stairs. It used to be the room where she kept a sewing machine, and his grandfather had a desk in the corner where he would keep their personal business. When she came home from the hospital, a group that assists the elderly had come over and moved furniture around. The small settee and desk were now in the corner of the den and her sewing machine and cabinet had been sold. A twin-sized bed, nightstand, and dresser as well as a comfortable chair now filled the room. There was no closet, but a standing wardrobe was in the corner and held her clothes.

Kissing her cheek after being assured that she could easily handle getting herself ready for bed, he headed upstairs.

He had planned on spending part of the evening making out a list of what he wanted to purchase at the home improvement store. But instead, as he lay in bed, thoughts of the family now sharing their backyard space filled his mind.

4

Ben rose early every morning, a habit ingrained from his years in the service. For the past several days since he'd been home, he'd made sure to be downstairs when his grandmother awoke so that he would be able to help if there was anything she needed. She was still independent, insisting on cooking him breakfast. But today as he crawled from bed, he noticed the sun was already streaming through the slats of the blinds on the window. Glancing at the old clock on the nightstand, he was surprised to see he'd slept later than usual.

Jerking on a pair of ratty sweatpants that hung below the waistband of his boxers, he jogged down the stairs. Rounding the corner, he headed into the kitchen. "Babciu?" Walking barefoot and bare-chested, he yawned widely while scrubbing one hand through his hair and the other scratched his stomach. Seeing his grandmother sitting at the table, he grinned widely. "Sorry I slept la—"

He blinked in surprise, his feet stuttering to a halt as

he realized she was not alone. A young woman was standing near the table, her eyes wide as her gaze moved from the top of his sticking-straight-up hair to his bare toes and back again. His gaze was feasting on her in the same manner. Her dark hair was pulled back into a low ponytail at the base of her neck. Her face appeared makeup-free, but her skin was luminous, and a healthy pink graced her cheeks. Her red t-shirt and blue jeans showcased her curves, and red slippers encased her feet. But as his gaze moved back to her face, it was her eyes that held him captive... deep blue... almost purple. Her pink lips parted, and the tip of her tongue barely peeked out to moisten her bottom lip.

"Benjamin!"

The sharp calling of his name jolted him from his perusal, and his attention shot toward his grandmother, whose lips were pursed as though he'd been caught sneaking a snack before dinner. "Yes, ma'am," he answered quickly.

"You can see I have a guest. She comes over when she can to check on me and to make sure I have what I need. She even brings groceries. I was just telling her about my grandson who is now here to help but had no idea you'd make such an *informal* appearance this morning."

Realizing his state of undress and unkempt appearance, he felt the rare heat of blush rise over his face. Living and working with his SEAL team for years, he hadn't given a thought as to what he looked like first thing in the morning when he rolled out of bed. Hell, half the time he'd slept in what he'd worn that day when on a mission. Even at the apartment he'd shared, he'd often walked out to one of his teammates saying goodbye to whatever half-dressed woman they'd picked up the night before.

Shit! He watched the woman's lips roll in, pressing together into a thin line, but was unable to tell if she was irritated or stifling a grin. Uncertain if he cursed aloud or in his head, he offered a quick chin lift as he mumbled, "Sorry. Excuse me." Turning, he walked out of the room toward the staircase, forcing his feet to go at a normal pace instead of trotting, determined to hang onto some semblance of dignity.

Upstairs, he pulled on a clean T-shirt, kicked off the sweatpants and jerked on a pair of jeans, slipped his feet into his boots, and ran a comb through his hair. Glancing into the mirror, satisfied that his appearance would now meet Babciu's acceptance, he jogged back downstairs. The woman must be a hired aide but his grandmother had not mentioned anyone coming over. Wondering if the beautiful woman would still be in the room, he reentered, breathing a sigh of relief to see she was now sitting at the table.

Babciu grinned as he poured a cup of coffee and walked over to the table, nodding her approval. "Much better. Now, Violet, let me introduce you to my grandson, Benjamin."

Reaching across the table, he took her hand, noting the fragile feel of her slender fingers. Almost delicate. And yet as she shook his hand, he also felt strength. "Violet, it's nice to meet you. Please, call me Ben."

"It's nice to meet you, too."

Now, he was struck with her voice. Soft, almost lyrical. And yet with an undercurrent of mirth. His gaze never left her face until he noticed she dropped her gaze to their still-held hands. Reluctantly letting go of her fingers, he cleared his throat and sat quickly, hoping to hide his immediate reaction. Usually able to control his cock, he tried to remember the last time he got laid. *Hell, it wasn't that long ago.* But looking at Violet, he had to admit, his last date—well, more like pick-up—had not been with anyone as elegant as she. He'd become tired of the bar scenes, but after their last mission, he'd felt restless and thought a romp between the sheets might do the trick. All it did was leave him feeling more restless and ready for a change.

"Benjamin!"

Blinking again, he jerked his gaze back to his grandmother. "Sorry, Babciu. What did you say?" Blushing again, he wondered if having red cheeks was going to be a permanent condition around this woman.

Anna looked toward an obviously amused Violet and shook her head. "What must you think? My grandson comes down half-dressed. And now when I talk to him, I might as well throw peas against the wall."

Casting a glance at Violet, he grinned at her wide-eyed expression aimed toward his grandmother. He chuckled and leaned closer. "She means I'm distracted. It's an old Polish saying."

Violet held his gaze, her smile still in place. "I... oh... I've never heard that."

"Peas don't stick to a wall—" he began before his grandmother interrupted and finished.

"And my words don't stick to him!"

Now, it was Violet's turn to laugh as she leaned her head back. Ben watched as the light coming through the kitchen window glistened in her dark hair and her eyes lit, their purple-blue hue mesmerizing. He wasn't sure if she was a homecare nurse that his grandmother hired to assist but hoped she would continue to come often.

Violet tucked a stray hair behind her ear. "Oh, my... I love that saying. I'll definitely have to use that on my kids. Half the time I think Lily and Charlie never listen to me!"

Jolting as though a bucket of cold water was dumped on top of him, Ben leaned back in his seat. *Whoa... kids... married.* He'd known a few guys over the years who would have gone for her anyway, but that wasn't his style. Time to push the attraction that had been clawing its way over him back into the box. Giving his head a little shake, he nodded politely and stood. "Babciu, I'm heading to the home store to get some supplies to begin working today. Violet, it was nice to have met you."

With that, he placed his mostly-full coffee cup into the sink and headed back upstairs.

By the time he fiddled with his list for the first round of renovations and came downstairs for the third time that morning, he breathed a sigh of relief to find his grandmother alone in the kitchen, her back to him as she washed out their coffee cups. He opened his mouth to speak until she twisted her head and peered at him over her shoulder, spearing him with her glare.

"Benjamin... you were rude to Violet. She's a good neighbor and has often come over to check on me. I did not raise you to be rude to a lady, and I cannot imagine the military taught you that, either."

She's the backyard neighbor... damn. "I'm sorry. I just had a lot to do today and figured the two of you might want to... um... talk... or something."

She didn't reply but her gaze was still narrow. Making a hasty exit, he gladly left the house to get to the home supply store before she took him to task once again.

Once there, he relaxed as he walked up and down the aisles. He'd made a list but decided to peruse the store for more ideas. When his grandfather updated the house years before, he'd accomplished a remarkable job, but with time, some of the renovations were outdated. Struck with a memory of wandering hardware and lumber stores with his grandfather slowed his steps. Looking around, he wondered if he could make a living renovating old houses. *Well, I'll find out by the time I get finished with this home.* He thought of the licensing requirements and determined to look them up that evening.

Looking at the cost of the new cabinets for the kitchen, he decided the ones she already had would be fine, they just needed refinishing. After buying a hand sander, wood stain, and topcoat, plus new knobs and handles, he considered the cabinets in the bathrooms. Deciding on paint, he stood at the color strips. His gaze landed on the strips that covered the range from deep blue to purple and Violet's eyes came to mind. He'd never seen eyes that shade. *Her husband was a lucky bastard to be able to peer into those eyes every morning.*

Blowing out a deep breath, he made his way down the line, settling on a soft grey paint for the powder room downstairs. Making more selections for the upstairs bathrooms, he finally headed to the plumbing section. Ordering new bathroom sinks, counters, and faucets, he was pleased when the total was less than the cost of what new kitchen cabinets would have been.

Parking on the side road for easier unloading through the door leading into the laundry room, he glanced toward the backyards, Violet's house coming into view. The paint was chipping on the wood frame around her back door and kitchen window. There was no deck and the concrete steps coming from the door to the ground sagged slightly on one side. With no patio, the grass was worn away at the bottom of the steps, probably creating a mud puddle when it rained. *Wonder why her husband hasn't fixed the place up since moving in?*

Shrugging, he once again shoved thoughts of the raven-haired beauty from his mind and focused on unloading his SUV. He'd arranged for a load of deck lumber to be delivered that afternoon and hoped the good weather held out so he could work on a rebuild. He wanted a larger deck that would lead down to a brick patio. The idea that he could enjoy the yard crossed with the reminder that his grandmother planned on selling her house.

Sighing, he couldn't help but grin as his grandmother walked over and patted his shoulder, appearing to have forgiven his abruptness of the morning. He kissed her cheek and spied a sandwich made from thick slices of bread and piled high with deli meat, cheese, tomatoes, and lettuce sitting on the kitchen counter. "Is that for me?"

"You need to keep up your strength if you're going to do so much work around here."

Snagging the plate with his meal along with one containing a much smaller sandwich to the table, he made sure she was seated comfortably before diving in.

"Did you get everything you went after?"

Wiping his mouth while he nodded, he then said, "Yes. I decided we don't need to put in new kitchen or bathroom cabinets. The ones that grandpa put in are in perfect condition. I thought I'd sand and refinish the ones in here, and then put a fresh coat of paint on the ones in the bathrooms. I bought new hardware, and that'll give them an updated look. I've ordered new sinks and countertops for the bathrooms, and those will get delivered next week. I went ahead and bought new faucets that I can put in at the same time."

"I can't imagine how much work this will be for you. Are you sure you want to do this?" She held his gaze and tilted her head. "I know you must've had other plans you wanted to accomplish when you left the military."

He shook his head slightly, swallowing the last bite. "Honestly, I left with little idea of what I wanted to do. During the entire drive from California, I thought about it. It's not always easy to take a military career and turn it into a civilian job. Especially not when I was a SEAL. I know some people go into law enforcement or security work, but I never considered doing that."

"Because of me?"

"No, no," he rushed, leaning forward to place his hand on hers as it rested on the top of the table.

"You don't owe me any debt, real or imagined, Benjamin."

"Oh, I know that. And yet I do. I owe you everything. But not in a way that I feel trapped. Just… well, just peaceful, I guess."

Their eyes stayed locked for a moment before a smile curved her lips, deepening the creases in her cheeks. She rose from the table and walked to the refrigerator to retrieve slices of apple pie. He watched her carefully, but she was steady on her feet and he knew she not only craved her independence but the physical therapist had insisted that movement was good for her. As she neared the table again, he took the plates from her and waited till she settled before diving into the sweet goodness, the cinnamon sugar exploding on his taste buds.

"So, what did you decide on the long drive across the country?"

He swallowed his bite, licking his lips. "It wasn't until I was actually standing in this house again that it hit me. Grandpa took such pride in the work he did on this house. I know he helped other people with their renovations. I realized it was something that I could do and enjoy as well."

Her face eased as he spoke, so he kept going.

"There are lots of fix-it shows on TV and tons of people are flipping homes now, but for real craftsmen who want to maintain the integrity of these old homes, I'm not sure many of them can do it."

Anna nodded enthusiastically. "Oh, yes. I saw the work someone did at a friend's house. After bragging about how they could improve it, they did an unsightly job and it had to be redone! Oh, the cost... it was terrible!"

"I'm looking into what I'd need to do to become licensed in this state. I might have to work for a contractor for a couple of years, but that'd be okay. I'd learn the tricks of the trade. And right now, I don't need the money." He caught her wide-eyed look of surprise. Chuckling, he amended, "Not that I'm independently wealthy."

She laughed and patted his hand again. "Well, I certainly know you didn't inherit a fortune from us."

He loved watching her laugh. His grandmother had a way to brighten any room, chasing away the gloom that might hang over him. It had been that way since she and his grandpa first took him in. "I inherited a fortune from you, you know. Maybe not what goes into the bank, but a fortune, nonetheless."

Her gasp resounded as tears filled her eyes. "Oh, sweet boy..."

He cleared his throat, hoping to speak past the lump that had appeared. "Are you sure you want to move?"

Her face fell as her gaze drifted to her hands resting on the top of the table. Sighing, she finally replied. "Most of my friends have left the area. I still see some at church, but none in the neighborhood. Well, I have Violet, who I care for, but none of my old friends. Many have moved in with their children or into retirement *villas*." She chuckled, her eyes now settled once again on him. "Isn't 'villa' a funny word… such an old-world term for the modern little houses that are built for older people? I suppose the phrase 'independent living facility' isn't any better. I'm not sure what is so *independent* about them."

He remained quiet, wanting to hear more about her desires and secretly wishing she didn't want to sell the house that held so many memories for both of them.

"But I know those places have activities to participate in. Things to keep my brain engaged and transportation to my doctors' appointments. Although, Bingo was never my favorite game," she added with a smile.

"Well, if you're not in a hurry, I'll be here until we get this place ready."

"Oh, my, Benjamin, you have no idea how glad that makes me!"

"I've got the time and the knowledge to work on the house and then think about either working for a contractor or working for myself. At least, that's the plan for now." Looking over his shoulder, he added, "And speaking of plans… I'd better get off my as—um… chair and get the rest of the materials in. I've got some wood being delivered this afternoon."

With that, he headed back outside, determined to make Babciu's home perfect. Excited to get started, he sighed heavily at the idea of selling the house he grew up in when the renovations were finished.

5

"Hey, mister! Whatcha doing?"

Twisting his head around, Ben spied a little girl and boy standing at the back fence staring at him. Actually, they weren't so much standing as having climbed halfway up with their feet tucked between the space in the chain-link and their arms hanging over the top, their fingers dangling. The girl was dressed from head to toe in varying shades of pink from her sneakers, shirt, and to the headband pushing her dark hair back from her face. Her blue jeans were the only nod to a different color. Next to her, the little boy was in mismatched everything, looking as though he threw on the first rumpled clothes he found on his floor... something Ben remembered doing when he was little. At least until his grandmother made him change.

Sighing at the interruption, especially when he thought his activity was obvious, he called out, "I'm building a deck."

He'd spent the first part of the week inside, sanding

and painting the bathroom cabinets while the rain kept him indoors. During a break in the weather yesterday he'd managed to rip out the old, small deck that extended straight from the back door. Not even large enough to set up a grill, it was barely more than an off-the-ground place to wipe feet before going indoors. Yesterday evening he sank the new supports into the ground, filling the holes with concrete after making sure they were level. He wanted to give them another day to cure, but with the sun now out in the cloudless sky, he'd spent the day cutting the lumber for the frame.

"It looks like it's going to be bigger than the one that was there."

"Yep." He offered a slight nod of his head and turned his back to them, the interruption causing him to relook at the measurements before reaching toward the piece of wood to place on the table with his circular saw.

"My name is Charlie. What's yours?"

Calling over his shoulder, he answered. "Ben."

"I'm Lily."

Since he'd already given his name, he thought perhaps he could keep working and just ignore the kids. As long as they stayed on their side of the fence, they wouldn't get in his way, and he wouldn't have to worry about them getting hurt.

"Mom says that you're Mrs. Popovich's grandson," Charlie called out.

"Yep."

"Mrs. Popovich showed us a picture of you one time. You were wearing your uniform. You couldn't really see your face very well because you were wearing sunglasses and had on a helmet. You also had a really big gun. My mom won't let me have a gun. But I thought your uniform was cool. I think that's what I want to be next Halloween. Do you think I can get a uniform in my size?"

"It would be a costume, Charlie, not a real uniform. Mom can find one at the store where we went last year."

"Well, when I get older, it can be a real uniform. I'll be bigger then," Charlie announced.

Having looked at his measurements three times— and forgetting them each time—it became evident that as long as Charlie was going to continue his running monologue interrupted only by snippets from his sister, Ben was never going to get the piece of wood cut correctly. Standing, he turned and faced the fence, irritation flooding him over the interruption. "So, do you kids have anything else to do? I'm kind of busy here."

"Nope," Charlie declared, his smile wide as he grabbed the top of the fence and leaned his head back, letting the sunshine beam down on his face.

Lily shook her head, but her gaze remained on Ben. "Can we call you Ben, or do we have to call you Mr. Popovich?"

Jerking slightly at the unexpected question, he opened his mouth to reply then realized he had no idea how to answer. "Uh... well, Mr. Popovich sounds like my grandfather. But... uh... maybe you should ask your parents what they want you to call an adult."

"Mom says we should be 'spectful," Charlie said, his gaze now back on Ben but his smile still as wide.

Lily huffed and turned her intense gaze from Ben to her brother. "*Re*spectful, Charlie. It's *re*spectful."

"Right! Mom says we should be reee...spectful," Charlie parroted with emphasis.

Getting a closer observation of the children, Ben spied a missing front tooth in Charlie's smile. He noted the thick, dark hair on both kids, so like their mother's. From this distance, he couldn't determine eye color but wondered if either had inherited Violet's unusual hue. *Or looked like their dad.*

With the week's rain chasing everyone inside, he hadn't seen Violet since their last encounter and still hadn't laid eyes on her husband. With another glance toward the peeling paint on their back door, he grimaced at the thought of the man who didn't take pride in where his family lived.

"Can we watch?" Charlie asked. "We've never seen anyone use a saw before."

"That's not true, Charlie," Lily corrected. "Mama had that man come in and fix the door that fell down and squished you."

"A door fell on you?" The question slipped from Ben's lips before he could stop himself. *At this rate, I'll never get the deck built.*

"It was right after we moved in last year. Charlie pulled open the closet door and the whole thing fell down on top of him, and he cried."

Charlie wrinkled his nose. "I was younger then. That's why I cried."

Inwardly grinning at the young boy's defense of his tears, Ben wondered why their dad hadn't fixed the door. "I don't blame you for crying. I'll bet that hurt." He looked back at the deck before facing the kids again. "I don't mind if you watch as long as your parents don't mind. You have to make sure to stay on your side of the fence so you'll be safe."

"Mom won't mind. It's been raining, and we haven't had a chance to be in the yard. Mom is cleaning the house today and told us to come outside. She said she'd like to get one mess cleaned up before we make another."

A chuckle slipped out, Ben remembering days when he was growing up and his grandmother was doing the same thing, fussing that he needed to clean his room and then not get under her feet when she was doing the rest of the house. Unable to hold back his curiosity, he asked, "What about your dad? Is he helping your mom today?"

"We don't have a daddy," Charlie said. "He died."

Ben's gaze shot from Charlie over to Lily's face, seeing a flash of something moving through her eyes. Gut punched at hearing their father was dead, the air rushed from his lungs as a deep memory of his parents hit him. He had no idea what to say to Charlie's matter-of-fact pronouncement and simply stood dumbly in place with his arms hanging to his sides.

"Mama says he's in heaven," Charlie continued. "I've seen pictures of him. Mama says I kind of look like him, but everyone else says I look like her." Tilting his head slightly to the side, he continued. "Who do you look like? You don't look like Mrs. Popovich. She's got gray hair!"

Still struggling with the news that their father was deceased, his gaze shot toward their back door as Violet stepped out of her house and waved. Her dark hair was pulled away from her face, and even though he couldn't see her eyes, he could imagine them after having only discovered their unique color once before. Black leggings encased her legs, which appeared long despite her petite stature. The blue top was not form-fitting but flattering nonetheless.

"Charlie, Lily! Stop bothering Mr. Popovich. Anyway, It's time for lunch."

Lily twisted her head around to look at her mother. "He said we can call him Ben as long as you say it's respectful."

Violet was too far away for him to see her face clearly, but he could swear her lips curved slightly as her shoulders drooped. She suddenly appeared so different to him. Not just a beautiful woman, but one who knew loss. Shaking his head, he attempted to dislodge the myriad of emotions and shouted, "It's fine with me. The kids aren't bothering me." Again, the words slipped out before he had a chance to think them through. *Jesus, didn't I just want to be left alone?*

The matter was taken out of his hands when Violet once more called the kids in for lunch. With a wave, the kids jumped down from the fence and raced toward her. She smiled and ruffled their hair before lifting her hand and offering a little wave toward him. Before he knew it, he was once again alone, his gaze still lingering on the now-closed door where they had disappeared.

His cheeks puffed as he exhaled a huge sigh, and he

turned back to the task at hand, continuing to work on the deck for a few minutes. He'd barely made any progress when his grandmother opened the door and called him to lunch as well. Shaking his head with a grin, he climbed the cinderblock makeshift steps and headed inside. Washing his hands in the sink, they sat at the table, bowls of pomidorow soup filled to the brim. The Polish version of tomato soup with noodles was one of his favorites and he dove in, barely coming up for air until he was scraping the bottom of the bowl.

"Goodness, Benjamin," his grandmother laughed. "You worked up an appetite out there."

"Sorry, Babciu, I guess I did." He leaned back in the chair, his gaze drifted out the sliding glass door, and he inclined his head toward the house across the yards. "What can you tell me about Violet and her kids?"

"Oh, I saw those darlings out by the fence. I'm sure they were fascinated with what you were doing." Finishing her soup, she pulled the platter of cookies closer.

He needed no encouragement and snagged several as he waited to hear what she had to say about the Mayfields.

"I told you the house sat empty since the owner went to jail, and I was afraid vagrants might take up residence. But one day, I saw a yard crew cutting the grass, and when I took a walk that afternoon, the For Sale sign in the front window was gone. I kept watching, and imagine my surprise when two children popped out the back door one day, running and playing in the yard."

He had no trouble imagining Charlie and Lily running around their yard, exploring every inch.

"I walked out to meet them and discovered that Charlie had no filter." She laughed, shaking her head. "In a few minutes, I learned that they had moved from another neighborhood in Hope City. Their mother had a job but was also taking some kind of classes. He was only five, had finished kindergarten, and would start first grade the next school year. His sister was almost nine and would be going into fourth grade."

He cleared his throat and shifted in his seat. "And their dad?"

Anna sighed, her smile falling from her face. "Yes. It didn't take long for me to ask about their parents, and Charlie announced that their dad had died."

"That's what he told me, too."

"I'm sorry, Benjamin," she said, reaching across the table to place her hand on his. "I'm sure it made you think of your parents."

He hefted his shoulders in a shrug. "It did but not with the pain I used to feel many years ago. It was more a sadness that any young child has to go through the death of a parent."

"I get the feeling that Charlie doesn't remember his dad very well and that Lily's memories are hidden a little deeper."

"And... um...Violet?"

Anna's brows lifted at the same time her shoulders did. "That's a bit more difficult."

Interest piqued, he cocked his head to the side in a silent question.

"I met her a few days later when she was in the back-yard with the kids. I offered a platter of cookies and we chatted. Such a lovely woman. We've become closer, so much so that I've babysat the kids occasionally when Violet was needed in her office and her regular sitter was unavailable. And Violet was right there after I had my stroke, coming over to assist with laundry, cooking, and cleaning. She's a wonderful mother but very tight-lipped about her deceased husband. I thought it might just be when the children were around, but she rarely speaks of him when it's just the two of us."

"Maybe it's too painful?"

She nodded. "I'm sure it was. But still, it was over three years ago. Since Charlie was only three, I think that's why his memories of his father exist in stories he's heard his mother and sister tell as well as photographs. Lily would have been almost six, her memories more ingrained." She stood and gathered the bowls, Ben jumping to his feet to assist. As they walked to the sink, she continued, "Violet doesn't talk about him, and I've respected her privacy. But she's mentioned that she doesn't have any real friends in the area, so I find myself wondering if perhaps she just hasn't found anyone to talk to."

They washed the dishes side-by-side in silence, each to their own thoughts. "You know," she began, "perhaps Violet would be able to talk to you."

His body jolted in surprise as he jerked his head down to see her staring up at him. "Me? Why me?"

"Because you understand loss. I do, too, of course, having suffered the loss of my son and his wife, and now husband. But you're closer to her age. You would be able to relate better."

"Babciu, I lost my parents, not a spouse. I have no idea what she's going through."

She lifted her shoulders in a little shrug. "Perhaps... but you can relate to the children. And through them, to her role as a mother."

They fell into silence again and his thoughts spun around. When he'd first met Violet the other day in this room, he was struck by her beauty. Hell, any man would have noticed the gorgeous woman.

But as soon as she mentioned the word 'kids', cold reality dumped on him. There was no reason to take his interest in her any further. He'd known some men in the military that would pursue and sleep with any woman and whether or not they were married didn't matter. But that had never been Ben.

Violet. Beautiful... a widow. With kids who'd lost their dad. He knew more than most the emotional impact of losing a parent as a child. *But what could I tell them? That loss won't touch them again?* That would be a lie. He'd lost his grandfather who'd been a surrogate father to him. Soon, even his grandmother would leave this house, taking more memories. He rubbed his hand over his chest wishing the ache would subside, hating the idea that nothing lasts forever.

6

Violet kept an eye on the clock in the corner of her computer as well as on the other employees in the office. She never left early but never wanted to be alone in the office with her boss, Fred Marsdale. Finishing the document she was working on, she sighed in relief as she hit *save* and shut down her computer. Seeing several others stand from their desks and begin waving good-bye, she stood as well. Before she had her purse out of her desk drawer, she felt the hairs on the back of her neck rise and knew Fred was nearby.

"Violet?"

She refused to look at him until she'd retrieved her purse, then turned to face him. Tall and thin, with his typical combover. She often thought that if he would simply cut his hair short, he would look younger. With his height advantage, he peered down at her, and as usual, his gaze dropped from her face to her chest. She longed to snap her fingers and remind him that her eyes were about ten inches higher. Clearing her throat loudly, she refused to plaster another fake smile onto her face, instead lifting a brow and tilting her head to the side. "Yes?"

"I wondered if perhaps you could stay a bit longer and help me organize the Barker files. Then afterward, we might be able to grab a drink."

A few more weeks and she would finish her degree, be free to look for a new job, and finally tell him where to shove his files. She opened her mouth, then hesitated. It would be so easy to tell him she was giving her notice. So easy to sling her purse on her shoulder, turn with a dramatic flounce, and stomp out. But she needed this job. At least until another one came along. One that would pay her bills, allow her to take care of her kids, and give them health insurance. But she was tired of avoiding his dinner and drinks invitations.

"Mr. Marlsdale, as you can see, the others have left the office and it's the end of the business day. I have a certain time that I need to pick up my children from their after-school care."

His nose wrinkled, an expression she was well acquainted with. Deciding to not give him a chance to rethink things, she walked around the far side of her desk, no easy task considering hers was jammed between several others. Turning sideways, she sucked in a breath to shimmy through the small opening between desks, which in truth would have only helped if a deep inhalation would take a few inches off her ass. But, making it through, she had a clear path to the doorway. "I'll see you tomorrow," she said, forcing enthusiasm into her voice, and with a little wave, made it out the front door. Once on the sidewalk, she breathed a sigh of relief and quickly walked to her car.

Driving home, she thought of her situation and grimaced. She couldn't wait to walk out. The reality, though, was that until she had another job, she couldn't afford to leave the one she had. But the idea of a job with more managerial duties loomed large in her mind. *Even a small company.* She had no dreams of working in a huge downtown high-rise, wearing fancier clothes and heels every day. *I just want to use my brain and be appreciated for what I accomplish.* A car horn honked behind her and she startled. Looking up, she saw the green light and grimaced once again. Pulling up in front of the rec center where Charlie and Lily stayed for a few hours after school, she sighed heavily, hoping the cares of her workday would drift away with her exhalation.

Waving to the rec center school coordinator, she smiled as her two dark-haired, bright-eyed children ran toward her. Offering squeezing hugs and kisses, the three of them piled into her car.

"I learned what we are in school today," Charlie said, bouncing in his booster seat.

Looking into the rearview mirror at his adorable chubby cheeks which she knew one day he would grow out of, she asked, "What are we?"

"I learned that a duo means two, and a trio means three! So we're a trio. You, me, and Lily."

She was glad she was facing forward in the driver's seat and he couldn't see the moisture gathering in her eyes. He was right. They were a trio—but not by choice.

Matt had been gone for years and the emotions surrounding his death had lessened a bit over time. *But we weren't supposed to be a trio.* She listened to her children's excited banter as they drove down their street. There were no parking places directly in front of her townhome, and not for the first time was she glad they had an end unit. Turning at the corner, she easily parked on the side street.

As the kids piled out of the car, she glanced forward. From this angle, she could see the back of Anna's house and had a perfect view of Ben working. His muscles flexed underneath his t-shirt as he lifted old pieces of lumber and tossed them into a pile. He turned and bent, and she had to admit the view of his jeans-covered ass was amazing.

"Mom!"

She startled and threw open her door, quickly climbing out. Embarrassed that she'd ogled him while hating being ogled by Fred, she followed her children to the front door. The narrow living room offered little space for messes, so the children had been taught to make it to the tiny dining room before they dumped their backpacks and headed into the kitchen.

"We've already had snacks at after-school care, so can we go outside and play?"

Bending to kiss Lily's head, she nodded. "Stay in the yard." As both children ran out the back door, she called out, "And don't bother Ben!" Following them to the door, she stared out the window as her children began kicking a ball back and forth in the yard. Her gaze automatically drifted to where Ben was still working.

Charlie ran to the fence and climbed up, his arms hanging over the top as he yelled his greeting toward Ben. Her breath hitched as she waited to see what Ben's response would be. She knew Charlie was fascinated with the presence of another man close by, one who was strong and kind.

Ben turned, and a smile spread across his face. "Hey, Charlie! Hi, Lily!"

Her breath left her lungs in a rush as she watched her children, thrilled to be acknowledged, hanging on the fence, their attention riveted by what was happening at Anna's house. As her gaze moved over Ben, she realized she was doing the same thing.

Ben's head lifted slightly, and now, his eyes were on her. His smile widened, and he waved. Her face flamed hot at being caught staring, but she lifted her hand and waved in return.

Forcing herself away from the back door, she took advantage of the few minutes of solitude while the kids were playing safely outside and another adult was present. Dashing upstairs, she pulled off her work slacks and blouse, toed off her sensible pumps, and wiggled her toes in relief. Slipping on a pair of leggings and a comfortable shirt, she ran a brush through her hair and pulled it away from her face with a clip.

The previous evening, she had breaded and baked chicken breast strips, and it didn't take long to put together chicken Parmesan, leaving out several of the chicken strips for Charlie. Tossing together a salad that would be mostly for her since Charlie also had an aversion to eating green things that looked like grass, so she heated green peas just for him.

Walking to the door, she started to call the children in when it dawned on her that Charlie was right. They were a trio. When Matt was alive, they were more. But now, she was satisfied with her little trio. *Even if, occasionally, I feel lonely in the midst of our chaos.* Squelching that thought, she walked out her door and across the yard to the fence.

As soon as she reached the fence, she placed her hands on each of her children's shoulders and bent to kiss first the top of Charlie's head and then Lily's. Standing, she started to call out Ben's name when she realized he was staring at her already. His gaze was on her face, and while she had no idea if he'd checked her out earlier, at least now his eyes were boring into hers, not her chest.

"Hello, Violet."

"Hey, Ben. I hope my children haven't been bothering you—"

"Mom!" Charlie complained, twisting his head around to look up at her. "We're not bothering him."

"Maybe to your way of thinking it's not bothering, but if you're keeping Ben from working, then it is."

"No, no," Ben called out. "They're fine... no problem at all."

"Mom?" Mimicking Charlie's position, Lily remained clinging to the fence while twisting her head around to look at Violet. "Mrs. Popovich has gone to her church meeting tonight. That means Ben doesn't have anyone to fix him dinner. Can he eat with us?"

Blinking, she quickly calculated the amount of dinner she'd fixed, wondering if it would feed the three of them plus a hungry man. Just as rapidly, the words *hungry man* hit her. Other than when her brother had visited, their trio hadn't had a man sitting at their table since Matt died. Even then, Charlie was still in a booster seat at the table.

"Mom?" Lily prodded, at the same time Charlie lifted his hands over his head and shouted, "Yay!"

Charlie's action caused him to wobble, and her hands snapped out to steady him, giving her a few more seconds to think of what to say.

"That's nice, but I'm good," Ben said. "I'm pretty self-sufficient, but my grandmother has leftovers in the refrigerator for me."

Considering the invitation had never made it out of Violet's mouth, Ben's generous reply gave her a reprieve at having to extend or rescind the offering of dinner with them. Suddenly, the idea of Ben heating leftovers by himself when she had food seemed ridiculous. *It's just a neighborly dinner.*

Lifting her gaze back to Ben, she smiled. "We'd love to have you eat dinner with us. Really. It's nothing fancy, but from the looks of what you've accomplished back here, I'd say you've been working all day. If you don't mind eating with a couple of rugrats, you're more than welcome."

While Lily and Charlie complained about being referred to as rugrats, she forced her gaze to stay on Ben. Warmth moved through her as his smile widened.

"Well, if you're sure I won't be intruding."

Waving her hand dismissively, she rolled her eyes. "Please, we'd love to have you." Nerves slithered through her stomach, and she wondered if her voice sounded as wheezy to him as it did to her.

"Well, let me wash up, and I'll be over."

His gaze moved past her toward her house, and she anticipated his thoughts. "You can just come to the back door." As soon as she spoke, she realized the fence between their yards had no gate. Opening her mouth to amend her instructions, he laughed.

"Don't worry about having no gate. I think I'm tall enough to jump it easily."

With his height, she had no doubt it would take little effort for him to hop over the fence, and the thought moved through her mind that she hoped she could witness him doing just that. With a wave, she called out, "It'll be ready whenever you get over." Assisting Charlie and Lily off the fence, she watched the kids run toward their house. Walking at a slower pace behind them, she wondered if Ben had gone back to work, gone inside his house, or was still standing there watching her. Not sure if she wanted him to be or not, she refused to look around until she stepped inside, turning only when the screen door shut behind her.

And yes, his eyes were still on her. She walked into the kitchen quickly, trying to ignore the fast beat of her heart. Thoughts of Ben were quickly swept away by the sounds of her children squabbling in the powder room as they fought over washing their hands in the sink. Pushing an errant strand of hair behind her ear, she rolled her eyes. *These leggings might make my ass look good, but I've still got a mom's body, a mom's concerns, and a mom's life.* Stepping in to referee the water and soap argument, she grinned at the children that centered her world and held her heart together. *Yeah, we're a trio... and that's fine with me!*

7

Ben stood at the sink in his grandmother's kitchen staring out the window. He'd taken a shower, washing off the sweat and grime from his workday. He'd changed into clean jeans before standing at his closet, trying to decide what shirt to put on. *Was a T-shirt too informal? Was a dress shirt too over the top?* Finally, in frustration, he'd grabbed a Navy polo and pulled it on, smoothing his hands over the material.

Now, he stared at the back of Violet's house. *What the hell am I doing?* He could tell Violet had been surprised when Lily suggested he come to dinner. Her deer-in-the-headlights expression was a definite giveaway. Ready to beg off, he was surprised when she smiled and extended the invitation. A polite refusal was on his mind, but when he'd opened his mouth, different words came out.

It's nothing. It's just dinner with neighbors. One beautiful neighbor and two kids. It wasn't as though he'd never been around kids, just not a lot. Back in California, being around Jeremy for holidays and times between missions, he felt like he related to kids. *Well, not as well as Zig.* The big guy had fallen head over heels for Jeremy and his mom, Andi. They were now a family, and it looked good on Zig.

His fingers gripped the sink's edge tighter. *Why the hell am I thinking of Zig and his new family?* Pushing away from the counter, he stalked to the back door, locking it behind him. He'd sent a text to Babciu letting her know he'd pick her up when her meeting was over. He knew she could get a ride with someone but figured he might need an easy way out if the neighborly dinner felt awkward.

Stalking through the backyard, he placed his hand on the top of a fence post and easily vaulted over. Now, he headed directly to the Mayfields' back door, having more dread for dinner than he did for a difficult mission. Lifting his hand to knock, the door was thrown open and Charlie looked up at him with a wide smile on his face.

"You're here! You came!" Charlie shouted.

Unable to keep from grinning at the little boy's enthusiasm, he nodded. "I said I would come, buddy."

"Charlie, stop shouting and let Ben come into the house." Violet appeared at the end of the kitchen counter, and Ben swallowed deeply as he stepped forward, two things hitting him at once. She was gorgeous with her deep blue eyes peering at him. And dinner smelled wonderful with Italian spices filling the air.

"Uh... it smells great. Thanks for inviting me." He

suddenly wondered if he should have brought something. A bottle of wine? *Maybe she doesn't drink with the kids around. Or at all.* Dessert? *Where the fuck would I have gotten dessert unless I raided my babcia's cookie jar?*

"Are you okay?" she asked, her gaze still pinned on him.

Jerking, he nodded. "Oh, yeah. I'm sorry I didn't bring anything with me."

Her smile brightened. "Goodness, I didn't expect anything. After all, we invited you."

He was saved from embarrassing himself further when Lily walked over and took him by the hand. "You can sit next to me."

"No, me!" Charlie shouted.

Rolling her eyes, Violet stepped in and said, "That is not how we act with company. Plus, there are only four of us at a square table. You can sit in your regular seats and Ben will be at the end, technically between both of you."

He was amazed at how quickly she dealt with their disagreement and how quickly the kids gave in to her suggestion. Still being dragged along, he looked over his shoulder. "Do you need some help?"

She waved him on and shook her head. "Charlie and Lily put the plates out, and I've already got the salad and bread there. I'll bring over the chicken parmesan." She turned back toward the kitchen counter and he followed Lily to the table.

Glad that his grandmother had drilled manners into him when he was younger, he placed his napkin on his lap. Violet set the main course in the middle of the table, and he waited to see how the family served themselves.

She looked at him and smiled. "Please, go ahead and help yourself."

The salad bowl was closest to him, so he started there. He looked toward Charlie, who made a face and shook his head. Uncertain, he glanced toward Lily. Violet walked back with a small bowl of green peas and chicken strips, placing them in front of Charlie.

"I think salad is yukky," Charlie declared. "I like the round peas better."

Violet bent low and whispered into her son's ear, "We don't say 'yukky' at the table."

Charlie's nose wrinkled again but he mumbled, "Sorry."

As Violet sat down, the rest of the food was passed around and served. She kept an eye on the kids, but they behaved perfectly. Catching his eyes, she smiled. "We're very casual, but I try to make sure the kids don't eat like heathens."

"I know what you mean. Babciu drilled table manners into me and then the military made sure I remembered them."

Charlie and Lily stopped mid-bites and stared. "Who's Bab—who?"

"Oh, sorry. That's my grandmother, Anna... uh... Mrs. Popovich."

"Why do you call her Bab-chu?" Lily asked, her eyes wide with interest.

"It's babcia... or babciu, depending on how it's used. Um... one is for talking about her and the other for talking to her. Um... it's Polish for grandmother." Seeing their wrinkled brows, he tried to think of how to explain further but ended up looking toward Violet for help.

"Kids, do you remember when we go to get pizza from Mr. Giovani? Sometimes, his nephew, Carlos, brings our pizza to the table. Well, he calls Mr. Giovani 'Zio' instead of uncle. It means the same but it's the Italian word for uncle."

Lily's eyes widened. "Isabella's grandmother calls her 'Nieta'. I thought she just didn't know her name, but Isabella told me that it meant granddaughter."

"Exactly, and Ben's grandmother is from..." Violet lifted her voice at the end in question, her gaze resting on him.

"Well, she was born here in Hope City, but her relatives came over from Poland. She spoke English but always called her grandmother Babciu, and it just stuck when I came to live with her. It's the only Polish word we use, other than some of her recipes."

Charlie sat up and grinned. "Like her cookies! She taught me ko-la-caki! It's a funny name but I love them!"

Ben chuckled and winked toward the young boy. "Me too." It seemed that the conversation eased after that, and the nerves that had tightened his stomach earlier disappeared. As they finished dessert, he leaned back in his chair. "That was delicious. Thank you."

Violet smiled as a light pink blush crossed her cheeks. "You caught us on a good night. With two young kids, dinner can often be whatever everyone is in the mood for. I try to have the kids eat well, but there are some nights it's just hotdogs and macaroni and cheese."

"After some of the meals I had on missions, hotdogs and mac and cheese sounds great."

"What are missions?" Charlie asked, his attention riveted on Ben.

By now, Ben realized that being around children was a kind of minefield. Shooting an apologetic grimace toward Violet, he fumbled, "Uh... it was my job. In the military. Jobs were... uh... called missions."

"So why didn't you get to eat good food when you are working?"

He swung his head from Charlie to Lily, who took up the questioning. "Didn't anybody fix your dinner?"

"When Mom doesn't feel like cooking, sometimes we order Chinese or pizza," Charlie threw out, looking very pleased to explain how dinner could work.

Rubbing his hand over his chin, he continued to blunder. "Well, uh... sometimes, it wasn't easy to fix dinner. Or call for takeout."

"So, what did you do?" Lily asked.

The idea of explaining to the kids that he'd been trained to survive on whatever he could catch and kill, even if it was insects, was probably not polite dinner conversation nor what Violet wanted him to expound on. His gaze found her again, and a sigh of relief eased from his lungs as she smiled and took over.

"Ben was in the military and had to travel to lots of different places to do his job. I'm sure that sometimes he was at a place where he could eat a nice dinner, and other times he wasn't. Do you guys remember the funny TV show you watched the other night about the family that went camping in a tent in the woods? They forgot their bag of food and only had their granola bars to eat. That's kind of what Ben had to do when they didn't have room to pack a lot of food."

Lily and Charlie accepted Violet's explanation, and he wondered how she so quickly managed to come up with an example they could understand. She sent them into the living room to finish their homework, and he leaped to his feet to help her clear the table. Rinsing the dishes in the sink, he handed them to her to be placed into the dishwasher.

"You're really good with your kids." He winced, wishing he could have thought of something more descriptive to say.

She laughed, her eyes twinkling. "They keep me on my toes, that's for sure. They're both at the age where they're filled with constant questions and manage to notice the most minute things to ask about while completely forgetting things that they do every day, like brushing their teeth or setting the table." She closed the dishwasher and leaned her hip against the counter.

He found that he wanted to stay, being much more comfortable than he imagined he'd be. Glancing at the clock on the stove, he startled. "I'm sorry to eat and run, but I promised Bab—my grandmother that I'd pick her up."

"Please, keep calling her Babciu. I think it was wonderful the children learned something new tonight."

"Thanks." Suddenly uncertain how to say goodbye, he was glad when she looked over her shoulder and called out to the children.

"Ben has to go pick up Mrs. Popovich. Come say goodbye and thank him for coming."

Charlie and Lily had been sitting in the living room whispering, but at their mother's call, they both raced into the room, throwing their arms around his waist while yelling, "Bye, Ben!" and "Thank you, Ben!"

Stunned at the hugs, he looked up to see Violet roll her eyes and reach out her hands to pull them back. He gave a quick shake of his head, and much to his surprise knelt and wrapped his arms around them. "Thanks should go to you guys. You and your mom fixed dinner for me."

As they let go, Charlie grinned as he looked up. "We'll be back outside tomorrow. Will you be there?"

"I'm sure I will be. On rainy days, I've got jobs inside to keep me busy, but on sunny days, I'll be working on the deck and patio."

"Okay, munchkins," Violet said, shooing them away. "Go finish your homework."

As the kids ran back to the living room, he walked to the door and turned to find Violet nearby. "Thanks again for dinner." He hesitated, the desire to stay longer battling with the need to leave.

"Goodnight, Ben. Tell Anna hello from us."

He nodded, glad that she had initiated the goodbye, and jogged down her steps and across the yard. With his hand on a fence post again, he vaulted over the fence. With the sixth sense developed as a SEAL, he looked back, not surprised to see her standing at the door watching. What did surprise him was her smile. It hit him in the chest like a shot. Blowing out his breath, he went through the gate at the side of their yard and headed to his SUV. Time to pick up his babcia… and push the beautiful Violet from his thoughts.

8

_____

The next morning, Ben was out early working on the deck, but his mind was more on the dinner the previous evening than what he was sawing and hammering. He'd decided not to mention having dinner with Violet and her kids, but as soon as Babciu noticed his meal was still in the refrigerator, she immediately asked him why he didn't eat. When he admitted that he'd had dinner with the Mayfields, she brightened considerably.

"We should have them over some time as well," she'd said, her smile wide. "Violet was so considerate after I had my stroke. She often brought food, and while I've taken her a few things, I've never had them over. That's very neglectful of me."

Chuckling, he'd shaken his head. "The last thing you are is neglectful of anyone."

She'd continued to question him about his visit with them until he finally escaped after she went to watch the news before bed. What he'd never admit to her was that after coming back home, he'd watched Violet moving about her kitchen through the window over the sink. She occasionally turned her head to the side and spoke or laughed, and he knew it was in response to Charlie and Lily. Their domesticity was something he'd never desired or thought would be his. Sex was a release only, and only after making sure his partner for the evening understood that was all it was.

That must be why the scene in Violet's house stayed on my mind. It simply reminds me of a time when I was a child and had a calm life here with my grandparents. But nothing could happen between them. Violet wasn't the kind of woman you had a fling with and being a neighbor made her even more off-limits. The last thing he needed to bring to Babciu's house was drama with a scorned neighbor.

A sound near the garbage cans at the edge of their yard caught his attention, and he turned to see what was behind them. A dog was nuzzling the cans, and he shouted, "Get out of there!" A stray dog knocking over the cans and scattering garbage up and down the street for him to pick up was not how he wanted to spend his morning.

The dog stopped and looked at him, cocking his head to the side. Medium-sized and solid brown with one ear sticking up and the other pointing down, he appeared to be trying to decide if Ben was friend or foe.

Standing to his full height, Ben stomped closer, prepared to wave his arms and yell to get the dog to move on. Instead, the dog plopped his bottom to the sidewalk and panted, his tongue lolling to the side. Seeing there was no collar or tag, he also noted the dog was thin. Not dangerously so, but enough that he wondered if anyone had been taking care of him. "Are you thirsty, boy?" Once again, words left his mouth before he thought them through. For a man who'd been a disciplined SEAL, the trait of blurting was strange. *First, Violet and the kids, and now, a stray dog.*

The dog stood again, walked over to the gate as though he knew exactly how to get in, and appeared to smile. Ben went inside and filled a large bowl with water, uncertain that the dog would still be waiting by the gate when he went back outside. But sure enough, the dog was still standing, its tail now wagging with vigor. He opened the gate, but before he was able to set the dish on the sidewalk outside the fence, the dog darted through, then turned and looked up at him. Sighing, Ben set the dish in the grass. The dog plunged his face into the water, lapping noisily, almost draining the bowl. Lifting his head again, he kept his eyes on Ben.

"I suppose that you're also hungry, right?" When he received the same brown-eyed stare, he went back inside with the bowl and opened the refrigerator door. Uncertain what to feed the dog, he grabbed some of the leftover beef stew that his grandmother had placed in a plastic container. Dumping a large portion into the bowl, he went back outside, chuckling as he saw the dog had moved closer and was sitting just at the edge of the deck. Setting the bowl down, he watched the dog attack the stew with as much enthusiasm as he had the water.

"That ought to satisfy you for now." He patted the dog's head, scratching his ears. Not wanting to leave the dog trapped in their yard, he walked over to the gate and opened it wide. "I'm making noise as I work. You can leave anytime you want."

He turned his back on the dog and continued measuring, sawing, hammering, and drilling. Getting into the rhythm of his build, he worked without interruption and was pleased to see the base of the deck almost complete. Until he had the railings and steps in place, he wouldn't allow his grandmother to come out but could already imagine her sitting on the deck, sipping tea in the mornings. He barely registered the slamming of a door before he heard shouts.

"Hi, Ben!"

"You got a dog!"

"Where did you get a dog?"

The afternoon had passed so quickly, he hadn't realized that Charlie and Lily had gotten home from school. He stood and waved, watching as they climbed the fence on their side, their arms hanging over the top.

"Ben! Your dog! Where did you get him?"

Charlie's shouts and Lily's questions finally hit him, and he turned around to see the brown dog still in the yard, now standing close to the kids, his tail once again wagging vigorously. Ben's heart jolted as he watched Charlie hang over the top of the fence, waving his small fingers toward the dog.

"Kids, stay back! He's a stray, and I don't want you to get hurt!" He strode across the yard, his gaze on the dog, ready to tackle it if it made a move toward the kids. They were on their side of the fence, but he had no doubt the dog could leap over it if he thought the kids might make a good snack. As he approached, the dog continued to wag his tail as though waiting for the game to continue.

"He doesn't look like a bad dog," Charlie said while keeping his fingers wisely away from the fence.

Ben patted the dog again, noting his happy disposition. "He just showed up today. I'm not sure if he belongs to anyone, but I did give him some food and water."

"He doesn't have a collar or tag," Lily stated. "Mom said we have to be careful around dogs that don't have collars and tags. But I agree with Charlie, he doesn't look like a bad dog."

"Well, your mom is right to be cautious. We don't know if he's had his vaccinations to keep him healthy."

Charlie piped up, his eyes as wide as his smile. "You can take him to the vet and get his vacin... um... shuns."

"Yeah!" Lily said, jumping up and down and clapping, which elicited jumping and barking from the dog. "Then he'll be your dog, and we can come over and play with him!"

Violet stepped out the back door, and Ben was grateful for the interruption, not knowing how to explain to the kids that the dog wasn't his to keep. She walked toward the fence, her smile making a good day seem better.

"Hello, Ben," she said as she reached the kids. Her gaze dropped to the dog at his feet, and her eyes widened. "You got a dog?"

Dropping his chin to his chest, he grinned, shaking his head slowly before looking back at the trio of expectant faces in front of him. "Actually, it's a stray that's conned its way into my backyard."

"A stray?" She sucked in her lips, her gaze worried. "Do you think he's safe?"

"Seems to be. At least, he's not aggressive. In fact, he seems really friendly. No fleas or ticks. Clean but a little thin."

"You should feed him some more," Lily pronounced.

"Honey, you need to let Ben decide how to handle the dog," Violet chided gently.

"But—" Charlie began, then quieted as Violet placed her hand on his shoulder and offered a little shake of her head.

"I did give him food and water earlier just so he wouldn't be hungry. I'll probably see if he's around tomorrow and check with the local veterinarians and shelter to see if anyone has lost him."

Before the kids could protest again, Violet redirected their attention. "Kids, do you want pizza or Chinese for takeout?"

"Whoa, sounds like it's a special night for you all," Ben said at the bright eyes of the kids.

Leaning closer, Violet admitted, "More like Mom is too tired to cook!"

"Ben is going to grill tonight," came his grandmother's voice from the back door. He swung his head around and spied her waving at them.

The idea of spending more time with the Mayfields was not what he wanted. Sure, the kids were cute, but they seemed desperate for attention when he was outside trying to work. And as much as Violet was off-limits, it was hard to tell his cock that she was just a neighbor only. He'd had to mentally go through the steps to take apart his weapon in an effort to tamp down the physical response to being around her.

With his back to the Mayfields, he tried to silently warn Babciu away with a bug-eyed glare, but she ignored him and continued. "We'd be glad for you all to join us. I've got lots of hamburgers and hot dogs, and Ben is a grillmaster!"

Before he had a chance to refute her over-exaggerated claim, the kids began cheering. Swinging his head back toward them, he caught Violet's grin sliding over her face. Blowing out his breath, he nodded. "Looks like we're grilling tonight."

Violet's stare was penetrating and he suddenly felt guilty at not making a more enthusiastic invitation. Just as it looked as though she was going to refuse, the kids began cheering again.

"Really," Ben said, holding Violet's gaze. "Please, come."

She nodded slowly before looking toward the back door. "Mrs. Popovich, what can I bring?"

"I've got plenty," came the reply before she moved back inside.

"I'll get the grill going," Ben said, knowing he had no choice but to acquiesce to his grandmother's commands. Looking down at the dog, he walked to the gate and slapped his hand on his thighs. "Come on, boy." When the dog dutifully trotted over, he let him out and then slipped back in, keeping the dog on the outside. Then, he walked to the kids and easily lifted them over into his backyard. Glancing at Violet, he said, "I just realized that you can't come in through the side gate since I put the dog out there." He reached his hands out.

"I'm sure I can make it. He seemed friendly enough with you."

"Yes, but until he's been checked out by a vet, I'd rather not take a chance."

She glanced at the fence and said, "Let me go change clothes and grab some potato salad that's in the fridge. I'm sure I can make it over the fence with a little help."

He watched her walk back toward her house, trying not to stare at her luscious ass. Blowing out his breath, he turned to the grill sitting to the side of the new deck. "Kids, be careful. With no rail, I don't want anyone to get hurt."

It didn't take long for the grill to heat and he grabbed the platter of meat. Hearing the kids yell for their mom, he turned to see Violet, now in jeans, sneakers, and a simple t-shirt walking toward him. He jogged to the fence, taking the bowl from her and setting it on the ground. "Stick your foot in the fence link and give a boost. I'll get you over." She did as he suggested and he spanned her waist with his hands, lifting her easily over the fence.

Her hands landed on his shoulders and she peered up, surprise on her face when he set her feet gently onto the grass. "Wow, I can't believe you lifted me!"

Chuckling, he reluctantly dropped his hands from her. "You're light." The words *you're perfect* ran through his mind, but he squelched them before they slipped out.

They walked to the deck and he placed his hand on her arm in caution. "The base is finished but with no rails, you should be careful."

Barking ensued at the gate, interrupting their moment. The kids ran over, watching as the dog barked and jumped up, enticing them to let him in. Charlie looked over his shoulder, pleading in his expression.

"Please, can we let him in? He was fine over here with Ben."

Violet and Ben walked to the kids, and Ben leaned over the gate, petting the excited dog's head.

"I'll let him into the yard when we go inside to eat," Ben said. It didn't take long for the burgers to grill and once Charlie, Lily, and Violet were inside the house, he let the dog have the run of the yard again. "Be good," he coaxed, the dog's happy nature worming its way inside Ben's heart.

Soon, they gathered around his grandmother's table, and conversation mixed with the sounds of the meal being consumed. The scene was domestic, but instead of making Ben anxious, he relaxed, enjoying the company.

"I thought you were just making a new deck, but I saw lots of paint cans in the bathroom," Lily said.

In the little time he'd spent in her company, he realized how astute she was. "Yeah... I'm working on the house."

Charlie sat up straight, his eyes holding interest. "What kind of work?"

"I want to fix up the bathrooms and kitchen. Some new light fixtures and fresh paint in some of the other rooms. This way, it will be all fixed up when my babcia decides to sell it."

"Sell it?" Lily squeaked, her eyes widening as she swung her head around to look at his grandmother. "Mrs. Popovich, are you moving away?"

"No!" Charlie shouted, his nose scrunched. "Then who will watch us when Mom's late? Or give us kolackzi cookies? Or— "

"Children, hush—" Violet began, shaking her head.

"Oh, my dears, I'm not moving right away." She looked at the others before her gaze settled on Ben. "While Ben is here, I'm perfectly content to stay where I am."

Lily stared at her French fries, appearing to carefully choose the next one to dip into ketchup before looking up and spearing Ben with her stare. "Mom says our house is falling down around our ears. You should come over and help Mom."

"Lily! Lord, give me strength!" Violet dropped her head back, her gaze on the ceiling... or maybe the heavens.

Ben chuckled at her actions, wondering how she managed everything on her own.

"Ben would be more than glad to take a look at what you need," Babciu said, causing his attention to swing from the sight of Violet's long neck and the pulse point visible at the base to his grandmother.

"Yay," Lily cheered, her voice somewhat subdued as she glanced toward her mother and managed to not wither under the cocked-brow glare.

"Ben, you certainly don't have to—" Violet began.

"No, no, it's fine. I can easily take a look at what you need… your house… what your house needs." Once more stunned that his mouth ran before his brain could put on the brakes, the heat of blush hit his cheeks.

Babciu and the kids chatted as they finished eating, and he was glad for the respite, noting Violet was quiet as well. Glancing to the side, he spied the dog lying patiently at the back door, occasionally lifting its head to peer inside.

"I'm glad you're keeping the dog," Lily said, her legs swinging freely as she sat.

"Well, I said that I'd check to see if anyone has reported him missing," Ben reminded. "That's not the same as saying that I can keep him."

"But you have to," Charlie insisted, his eyes wide. "He can guard our backyards to keep the bad man out."

The forkful of salad halted on the way to Ben's lips as he turned his attention to Charlie. Before he had a chance to ask what he meant, Violet beat him to it.

"What bad man, sweetie?"

"The one who comes at night." Charlie kept eating, seemingly unaware of the adults at the table staring at him.

"He says he sees bad men at night." Lily shrugged before adding, "But he's right. The dog can keep them away."

"Honey, I didn't know you were having bad dreams." Violet leaned over and patted Charlie's arm. "You should always tell me when you get scared."

"Well, if Ben has a guard dog, then no bad men can get us, right?"

Ben's breath caught in his throat as Charlie turned his trusting eyes toward him. "Sure," he agreed, the word flying from his mouth. As soon as the promise was out there, he inwardly winced. *I was just thinking that nothing lasts forever, and here I am promising to keep all the bad dreams away.*

"Yay!" the kids cheered, fears forgotten as their excitement spilled over and they began to ask about the dog.

"Well, first, Ben has to check to see if the dog belongs to anyone," Violet cautioned.

For an instant, he sighed in relief at the thought that the friendly dog was probably someone's pet, and he wouldn't keep it. But the happiness on the kids' faces caused him to immediately change his mind and hope that perhaps it would be a good pet to have. "We'll see. Plus, I have to make sure it has its vaccinations."

"Perhaps Mrs. Popovich doesn't need a dog—" Violet continued.

"I think it's a lovely idea to have a dog," his grandmother said, winking at Ben before bestowing her smile onto the kids.

"If you do get to keep him, can we help name him?" Lily asked.

Violet shushed her, but Ben nodded, gaining smiles from the others. "Sure, we'll all figure out a name."

"Well, it looks like if no one is looking for him, we might have a dog."

He observed the twinkle in his grandmother's eyes and shook his head, wondering how dinner turned into the possibility of adopting a pet and agreeing to check on Violet's house.

At the end of dinner, he was the first to walk outside to hold the dog so the Mayfields could walk to the side gate and step onto the sidewalk before moving to their gate and entering their own backyard.

"You know, it would be easier if we had a gate between our backyards," Lily stated in the matter-of-fact way that Ben was beginning to associate with her. The little girl waved goodbye and headed into their house after Charlie.

He let the dog run in the yard again now that the kids were away. Instead of following the kids into her house, Violet walked toward the fence between the two yards. The dog jumped with joy as she leaned over and patted his head. *Lucky dog.* Hustling over, he stopped close enough that he caught the scent of flowers and wondered if it was her shampoo. As she stood, his eyes locked on her porcelain face so close to his. Her tongue slipped out, moistening her lips. Now, his gaze was zeroed in on her lips. He was so close that if he leaned over further, he could see if her lips were as soft as they appeared—*fuck, what?*

"I wanted to tell you how nice it was for us to have dinner with you and Anna tonight," she said, her gaze holding his. "Since moving here, we've been a bit isolated. The kids have friends at school and in their after-school care program, but other than playing at the park across the street, they're mostly just here in our house or backyard."

Dragging his attention to her words and off her

beauty, he nodded. "They're great kids, Violet. You're doing an amazing job by yourself..." Suddenly the words became stuck as he struggled with how to say what he was thinking without drawing attention to her widowhood.

"It's okay, Ben. You don't have to be embarrassed to mention that I'm a single mother. And I have to agree. They are great kids, although I never know what's going to come out of their mouths. Please, don't feel like you have to take a look at our house."

"No, it's all right. I'm more than happy to. I'm not a contractor, but there's a lot I can do."

She looked up at him with her lips curving and the delicate scent of her floral shampoo wafting by, and with only the fence between them, the desire to give in and lean forward—

"Woof!"

Blinking, he jolted as the dog jumped up and placed his front paws on Ben's thigh. At first, frustrated at being cock-blocked, he realized the dog saved him from making a mistake. *She doesn't need a mess like me... washed up SEAL, no paying job at the moment, and sure as fuck not daddy material.*

He stepped back from the fence and watched as she did the same. "Well, I'll see you... I guess tomorrow," he mumbled.

"Please, let us know what the vet and shelter say about the dog. I know the kids will be anxious to find out."

Nodding, he was glad to have an excuse to see her

tomorrow despite knowing it probably wasn't the smart thing to do. "Yeah, absolutely. Good night, Violet."

With a little wave and another smile, she turned and walked to her back door. Waiting until she was safely inside, he turned toward his own house. With the dog at his heels, Ben laid an old towel on the deck, offering the dog a bed. With a last look at Violet's house, he sighed and headed inside.

9

"Violet?"

She winced, then cleared her expression before turning around. Her usual mental preparation for Fred's approach had fallen by the wayside considering she'd spent much of the day with Ben on her mind.

When she'd first met Ben, she was simply glad that Anna had her grandson staying with her. But neighborly consideration was soon supplanted with a healthy dose of lust.

Benjamin was handsome but in a way that was different than the men she met at work. The ones who spent an inordinate amount of time in front of the mirror, with product in their hair, nails buffed, and even if dressed casually, she knew their clothes had been carefully picked out and coordinated. Ben gave the appearance of a man who ran his fingers through his hair after a shower, shaved when he was in the mood, and put on clean work clothes meant for the physical labor he was accomplishing. And she found him not only attractive but fulfilling a daydreaming fantasy that had settled into her mind. *Lord knows it's been a long time since I've been with a man.*

And now, with Fred standing right next to her desk, she looked up, swallowing the sigh that threatened to erupt. "Yes?"

"I'll need you to stay later today because we have the Rollins' report that must be finished. I was delayed in working on it but will have it soon and will need you to look over the figures before we send it out."

She opened her mouth to deny the ability to stay late, but he jumped in and continued.

"You've been unable to stay late because of your classes, which I've been very accommodating with."

Gritting her teeth so hard she was surprised they didn't crack, she wanted to remind him that his uncle had promised she could have time off for her classes which she seldom took since she worked on the online classes in the evenings and the in-person classes were usually on Saturdays. "I didn't realize that not staying late was considered negative for my job performance considering I get my work completed during the regular office hours."

"Now, now, Violet, don't get upset. I'm sure your next employee evaluation will be just as glowing as always," he said with his hand rubbing her shoulder.

Turning in her chair to face him and causing his hand to drop, she stood, not wanting him looming over her.

"But we must have this report finished and sent out

today. It's in the contract. I'll order dinner in, and I'm sure we can have it done quickly."

Not wanting to be alone in the office with him, she said, "Robert has also worked on the report. I assume he'll stay as well?"

Fred's lips pinched, but Robert came to her rescue.

"Sure, I'll stay. I'll call my wife and tell her to expect me late," Robert said, winking at her behind Fred's back.

"Fine," Fred agreed, "but I'll expect everyone to chip in for their own dinner."

As he turned and stalked off, she looked at Robert and mouthed, *thank you.*

"You know, Violet, you shouldn't have to avoid him."

"I know, but I need this job for now."

He nodded his understanding. "How much longer until you graduate?"

The knot in her stomach loosened, and she grinned. "I have finals in my last classes in another week, and then that's it."

"Are you going to look for a new job?"

She glanced toward Fred's now-closed office door before shifting her gaze back to Robert but still lowered her voice. "I don't think I have a choice. Ever since Fred took over for his uncle, my bookkeeping job devolved into more of a glorified receptionist. I hope to find something where I can combine my bookkeeping skills with the managerial degree." She shrugged while holding his sympathetic gaze. "But I need the salary and insurance from here until I find something else."

Robert headed back to his desk, and she sighed again. Staying late meant she needed to have the kids miss after-school care and go to Anna's house. Since Anna's illness, she'd rarely used her to keep her children, but Anna insisted she wanted to. Calling her, she was glad when Anna picked up the phone.

"I'm so sorry to bother you, but I've got to work late and can't get out of it. If I call the school and have Charlie and Lily dropped off at your house, can you watch them for just a little while?"

"Oh, Violet, of course. And don't worry about a thing. They'll be fine with me and Benjamin until you get home."

The idea of Ben being saddled with her rambunctious kids made her cringe, but unable to come up with another plan, she agreed. "I'll be home as soon as I can get away," she promised. Receiving Anna's vow of delight at the kids visiting, she disconnected. Her earlier daydream fantasy about Ben disappeared completely. *Nothing like a man having to deal with kids—and their mess of a mom—to shoot down any thoughts of romance.* Snorting, she turned to the ringing phone on her desk and answered. *Yep... reality strikes again.*

Ben took the dog to the veterinarian that morning and talked to the local animal shelter. No one had reported a dog missing that matched the description. The veterinarian found no chip and completed an examination, declaring the dog healthy although underweight, and approximated his age to be eighteen months old. Upon their suggestion, he agreed to have the necessary vaccinations given.

All during the examination, the dog was happy and content, tail wagging and tongue lolling. Snapping on the newly bought leash, they walked out and he looked down and chuckled. "Looks like you're coming home with me."

Once at home, Babciu wanted to let the dog inside the house, but he managed to convince her it was not a good idea. "I'm going to be working outside and can't keep an eye on the dog. We don't know if he'll chew on furniture or is housetrained. We need to leave him in the yard until I can spend a little more time with him."

At first, the dog sniffed all around the yard then settled nearby, curling up on the old towel. Ben managed to get the posts and rails cut for the deck and screwed into place. Giving each one a shake, he was satisfied that they would be sturdy enough for everyone's safety, including the kids. *The kids?* Giving his head a shake, he wondered when he started thinking of Charlie and Lily's safety.

Standing, he thought back to what Lily had said about the closet door falling on top of Charlie and how Violet had to call in a handyman. The idea of their house not being safe grated on him. And the idea of an unknown man in there also did not sit well. *If I want construction experience, her house is as good as any to get it.* Satisfied that his desire to assist Violet with her house was purely a good career decision as well as being neighborly, he went back to work.

Finishing the deck rail, he moved inside. By midafternoon, he'd sanded, cleaned, primed, and painted the bathroom cabinets in both upstairs bathrooms as well as the powder room.

Just as he finished, a commotion erupted from downstairs, and he hurried to see what was happening. Stepping into the kitchen, he spied his grandmother laughing while clapping her hands, Lily and Charlie jumping up and down, and the dog leaping from one to the other, getting ear rubs in the middle of the kitchen floor.

"I thought we were going to keep the dog outside," he said, his voice grumpier than he meant.

Lily and Charlie looked up at him, their eyes wide. "I'm sorry," Charlie said. "We saw him in the backyard and thought he'd like to come in."

The kids' apologetic expressions as well as Babciu's narrow-eyed glare caused guilt to spear inside. "No, no, it's fine," he assured, patting his thigh and grinning as the dog trotted over.

"Violet called and said her boss is requiring her to stay late and asked if the kids could get off the bus here. Of course, I agreed and she let the school know. I'm on their emergency contact list."

He nodded, not surprised she had volunteered to watch the kids.

"So, can you keep him?" Lily asked, her hands moving over the wriggling dog.

"Yeah, I guess so. He got a clean bill of health and his vaccinations." He grinned at the dog basking in the attention.

The children cheered again before his grandmother

corralled them to sit at the table for their snack. Ben turned to go back upstairs to finish the last coat of paint on a cabinet when he caught Charlie sneaking a bite of cookie to the dog.

"I'll take the dog outside while you eat. We don't want him to get sick." Ben grabbed the dog's collar and led him through the door. Once outside, he bent down and said, "Stay here and be good. I've got a feeling those kids would spoil you rotten."

The dog grinned, his tongue hanging out, but laid down on the deck. Back inside, Ben headed toward the downstairs powder room only to find Charlie standing at the sink with paint on his hands.

"I'm sorry… I thought the cabinet was pretty, but when I touched it, the paint came off on me!"

"No worries," he sighed, helping the little boy get his hands clean. He grabbed his paintbrush and carefully painted over the small handprint. Looking at Charlie's excited face as well as the swipe of dirty dog paw print on the bottom of his shirt, he sighed. "Um, do you have an extra shirt in your backpack? I hate for your school clothes to get messed up."

Charlie shook his head and wrinkled his nose. "I can go home and change. Mom usually has me get out of my school clothes as soon as we get home."

"I can't let you go over by yourself—"

"Come with me. Then I can show you my room!" Charlie ran out of the bathroom, shouting, "Lily, Ben is coming over to our house!"

His cheeks puffed out with a heavy exhalation as he followed more slowly into the kitchen. Babciu's smile was beaming at him. "I thought he should change clothes."

"What a wonderful idea," she said. "You can take a look around to see what needs to be fixed while you're there. Lily can go, also, to make sure Charlie gets what he needs."

Before he knew what was happening, he was heading across the backyard, kids in tow and the dog jumping around their legs. He lifted Lily over the fence first, then turned to swing Charlie into the air. Leaping over himself, he glanced back at the dog, who had plopped his bottom to the grass and stared longingly at them.

"I hate to leave him by himself," Charlie said, looking back at the dog while walking forward, his feet stumbling.

"We need to name him," Lily pronounced, then halted, her gaze turned up toward Ben's. "Although, Mom said we need to let you decide." She scrunched her nose, and he felt her sharp perusal.

"Uh... I don't mind if you decide on a name," he said, then immediately wondered if that was a good idea. The thought of having to call his dog something ridiculous ran through his mind, but seeing Lily's face light up, he didn't have the heart to take back his offer.

Reaching the back door, he pulled out the Mayfields' spare key that Babciu had given him. Once inside, the children ran upstairs to change clothes, and he glanced around the kitchen to see what Violet might need in the way of repairs or refurbishing. The kitchen cabinets were older but well-built. Glancing at her appliances, it was obvious the dishwasher was ancient, but her stove and refrigerator were fairly new. The floor was clean-but-faded vinyl and certainly could be updated.

Walking to the powder room under the stairs, he noted the sink had a drip and was chipped on the edge. The cabinet door was hung crooked, the wood faded. The toilet appeared to be in good condition although old with rust stains in the bowl.

"Ben! Come see my room!"

Charlie's voice carried easily down the stairs and Ben chuckled, remembering many times that his grandparents had to remind him to use his inside voice. "Okay, Bud, I'm coming. Uh... Lily? Are you... uh... all dressed?"

Gaining an affirmative, he ascended the stairs, nervous about being in Violet's home without her. The kids were in the hall, bouncing on their toes, now wearing their play clothes. He followed Charlie into his room, seeing that Violet had decorated it as a little boy's haven.

"I used to have dinosaurs on the walls of our old house, but for my last birthday, I asked Mom if I could have race cars."

"Looks good," Ben said, appreciating the decorating while noting the strip of foam that had been placed at the bottom of the window to keep the cold air out. *New windows can be added to the list.*

A framed photograph sitting on the nightstand caught his eye. It was a picture of a man holding a toddler with a little girl leaning against his leg. Dark hair with a wide smile. *Their dad.* Violet wasn't in the picture, and he assumed she must have been the one behind the camera taking the shot.

After checking the strength of Charlie's closet door, he was led into Lily's room. Her room was an explosion of little-girl and not-so-little-girl. There was a poster of a young actor from a show that Ben had seen advertised, plus a boy band that he instinctively knew their music was shit. It was displayed next to a pink and purple poster of a unicorn. A bookcase held neatly stacked books, while a few stuffed animals sat on her bed. She talked nonstop while he checked her window and closet door as well.

It was hard not to notice another frame on her nightstand, similar to the one in Charlie's room, the same smiling man with Lily tucked into his arms.

"That's my dad." Lily's proclamation held a wistful tone. "I don't remember him very well. Charlie doesn't at all, so Mom says the pictures will remind us that he loved us."

"I'm sure he did," Ben said, his voice soft. He remembered his grandparents made sure he had a photograph of his parents in his room at their house as soon as he moved in with them. His heart pounded at the expression on Lily's face, and he wondered if it mirrored his own several years after his parents died. Not raw emotion... but a deep sadness that was never far from the surface.

Having no idea what to say, he started to back out of the room but halted when he backed into Charlie standing in the doorway. Halting quickly, he looked down to see Charlie looking toward his sister.

"I asked Mom why Dad had to die cause it's not fair that my friends have dads and I don't," Charlie said.

Ben's chest depressed as the air left his lungs. He remembered asking his grandparents the same thing.

"She just said that some things aren't forever." Charlie sighed then looked up at Ben. "I still don't get why a dad can't be forever."

Ben opened his mouth but no words came out. How the hell could he explain it to Charlie when he had no fuckin' idea himself?

"Do you have any kids?" Lily asked, drawing his attention over to her. She stood with her arms crossed and her penetrating gaze hid deep thoughts.

"No… uh… no kids."

"Don't you like kids?" she asked, her eyes wide.

"Sure… I… uh… like kids just fine."

"Oh, I get it," she giggled. "You're not married."

"No," he admitted, hearing another giggle from behind him, and he turned to see Charlie crinkle his nose. Glad that the kids had moved from their heavier emotions but not sure he wanted to be the focus of their attention, he tried to step out of the room again.

"Do you got a girlfriend?" Charlie asked.

"Ah… no… listen, kids, let's go back downstairs—"

"I don't either, but Rosalie is always trying to kiss me at recess. I don't even like kissing!"

Eyes wide, he placed his hands onto Charlie's shoulders and mumbled, "Well, you're a little young for kissing."

"Yeah, but you're not," Lily stated, her hands now landing on her hips, a stance he'd seen Violet take when she was exasperated with her kids. "Why don't you have a girlfriend?"

"I... I haven't met anyone... well, that's to say, I haven't been in town long... but not that I was looking..." Feeling a drop of sweat run down his back, he recognized an inquisition worthy of Babciu. "Listen, we need to get back to—"

"You should look at the bathrooms up here, too," Charlie said, walking into another room. "Our cabinets aren't nicely painted like yours."

Ben wondered if it was possible to suffer whiplash from their quick-changing conversation topics, although he was glad to be off the topic of his lack of a girlfriend, which only served to make him think of their mom in a definitely non-mom way. He followed Charlie then skidded to a halt when he realized he was in Violet's bedroom. Backing up again, he ran into Lily behind him. *Damn, I can't get away!*

"Her bathroom is over there." Charlie pointed to an open door.

"Guys, I'm not sure your mom would appreciate me being in her room without her knowing—"

"She won't care. She's always complaining that the shower drips and her toilet flushes weird." Charlie led the way into the bathroom and against his better judgment, Ben followed.

The space was not large but neat. Violet's makeup was in a storage basket on the counter next to the sink. A wicker rack contained clean, folded towels. The scent of her floral shampoo permeated the room, and he dragged in a deep breath, loving the smell. He pulled back the shower curtain over the tub and noted the drip from the showerhead. The sound of the toilet flushing behind him caused him to turn quickly, seeing Charlie grinning.

"See… it makes a funny noise," Charlie said, laughing.

Having seen enough to know what could be accomplished in the room, he led the way out, peering around at Violet's bedroom despite his best intentions to get out quickly. Just like the bathroom, the room was neat. The bed was covered in a deep purple and blue comforter, matching pillows at the head. A dresser sat on one side, a small jewelry box sitting on top. He'd never seen her wear much jewelry, just small silver hoop earrings or studs.

A framed photograph on her nightstand caught his eye. It was of Violet, Charlie, and Lily. She was smiling, her arms around the children. It appeared to be fairly recent, which meant her husband was already deceased. Curious, he glanced around the room but noticed the other pictures that lined the dresser mirror were also of Violet or the children only. None of her husband from years past… no wedding pictures, none with the whole family.

Suddenly, he felt like an interloper invading her private space and winced, turning quickly. "Come on, kids. I shouldn't be in here without your mom's permission. Let's go back to my house."

Grateful they didn't argue, they bounded down the stairs, now excited to name the dog. Ben followed but cast his gaze toward the living room, once more noting there were no pictures of the whole family together. *Where are their dad's pictures?*

"Come on, Ben! The dog is waiting for us at the fence!"

He jogged after Lily, seeing Charlie already bolting out the back door. Making sure to lock the door behind him, he followed them to the fence, grinning at the dog now jumping up and down, its tail wagging in circles.

Charlie had already climbed the fence and dangled his hands over the other side, laughing as the dog licked his fingers. Ben scooped Charlie over, setting his feet on the grass next to the dog before turning back and doing the same with Lily. Hopping over himself, the group headed to his back door, the dog determined to come inside with the others.

While his grandmother settled the kids at the table to start their homework, he jotted down notes from Violet's house, making a list of what needed to be completed. His pen stopped scribbling as he thought of the photographs in the kids' rooms providing a daily remembrance of their father... and none in Violet's room.

Laying down his pen as he struggled to finish the list, he turned to see Lily staring at him, an indescribable expression on her face giving no indication of her thoughts—as though she could see the interest he tried to hide.

Irritation roared through Violet as she walked out of the office, waving to Robert and barely nodding toward Fred. Robert's presence kept Fred from asking her for drinks, something she simply would have denied as she always did. Her stomach growled because she refused to spend money on sandwiches for dinner when she could eat at home. Fred had scowled at her recalcitrance, but she had worked while he ate, telling him that she was leaving as soon as she had her part of the report finished.

She tried to hurry but the traffic seemed to mock her efforts to get home and relieve Anna of Charlie and Lily. She hoped the evening had not been too strenuous. She'd never had to rely on Anna to babysit often, but on the occasions she had used her, it appeared that Lily, Charlie, and Anna all enjoyed themselves. The kids saw her parents when they visited, but Matt's parents were more of the send-a-card-with-money grandparents. While she would never deny them the chance to be with the kids, they'd moved to Florida to be nearer Matt's sister. In truth, that was fine with her. Less pretending that all had been normal.

Shoving those thoughts to the side, she focused on finding a parking spot near her house, then decided since she had to pick the kids up at Anna's, she might as well pull around to the side road that ran along their combined backyards.

While Anna was much stronger, Violet was glad that Ben was home also to assist. Just as the thought of him struck, her lips curved. She hadn't allowed herself to be attracted to a man since... well, for a very long time. He was handsome, but she knew that there was more to a man than appearance. While he'd never given any indication that he was interested... A snort escaped. *Interested? He could get any woman he wanted. He certainly wouldn't look twice at a single mom with a mortgaged house that needed repairs.*

Finally, she pulled into a parking space next to her townhouse. The sun was setting, giving more evidence that she'd missed her evening with her children. Now parked, she hurried out of her car and headed toward Anna's house, entering the backyard through the side gate. She noted the Popovich garbage cans neatly sitting on the sidewalk just before noticing hers were sitting outside her gate, too. Crinkling her forehead, she wondered if Ben had taken out her garbage cans.

Turning, her attention was diverted by the sight through the sliding glass door and her feet stumbled to a halt. The dark evening around her only served to illuminate the lighted vision through the glass. Lily and

Charlie sat at the kitchen table, their backpacks neatly pushed to the side, making room for a board game. Glasses of milk and a platter of cookies sat nearby, and Violet knew that the children would've been fed a nutritious dinner, making sure they ate before they had dessert.

Charlie was on his knees in the chair, leaning over the table, his head thrown back in laughter. Lily, still a child and yet soon to be a tween, was grinning at her brother. Sitting on one of the kitchen stools at the counter was Ben, a pen in his hand. His attention was not on whatever he'd been writing but on the three at the table, a wide smile on his face. His jeans were molded to his thighs, and the black T-shirt was pulled across his chest and upper arms. His dark hair was pushed to the side as though he shoved his fingers through it. She wondered if it was as soft as it looked.

With one hand on the new railing, her other hand lifted and pressed against her chest, her heart squeezing. For a moment, it was so easy to pretend. Pretend that this was her home. Pretend that this was where she would come every evening, knowing her children were well-cared-for. Pretend that Anna was the constant grandmother figure that her children deserved. Pretend that Ben was a loving, caring father. And that he and she were—

"Mom!"

Startling, she blinked and saw Charlie staring through the glass door toward her, one hand lifted, waving wildly. The others in the room twisted around, smiling as they saw her. Hurrying up the steps, she reached out to open the door when suddenly, Ben was on the other side, sliding it open. She held his gaze and smiled.

"Welcome home," he said, his deep voice gliding over her.

Before she had a chance to respond, the children rushed over with hugs, both clambering to tell her about their day. The dog that had been relegated to the yard was obviously inside, jumping and barking along with the children, the cacophony almost deafening. And yet so welcoming. Something she hadn't had in a very long time.

Leaning over, she enveloped Lily and Charlie in hugs, kissing the tops of their heads while exclaiming how glad she was to see them. "Please, tell me you were good for Mrs. Popovich."

Both jumped up and down, exclaiming, "We were!" Lily launched into a litany of what all they had done. "We finished our homework, we helped with dinner, and then we ate, we played with the dog, we made cookies, and we were just playing a game."

Not to be outdone, Charlie continued to bounce up and down as he shouted, "I got paint on my hands, and Ben took me over to our house so that I could change clothes. And then he looked around!"

She glanced up toward Ben, her brow furrowed but noticing a blush move across his face. "Um... looked around?"

Before he had a chance to reply, Lily piped up, "We told him to take a look around to see what he could fix."

Standing straight, she shook her head while holding

his gaze. "Ben, you don't have to do anything in my house. I would never expect that."

He shrugged. "It's not a big deal, Violet. I'm at the home store all the time now anyway with what I'm doing here. It's easy to do a little work on your place as well."

The dog pushed its way between her and the children, wanting attention, and she leaned down to ruffle his ears. She twisted her head toward Ben and away from her kids before she mouthed, *"Is he staying?"*

Ben laughed and nodded. "The vet said no chip was found and the shelter hasn't reported him missing. So, he's had his shots and looks like we've got a dog."

She sucked in a quick breath at the way he said *we've*, the sound of that simple word making her feel less alone.

Charlie pulled on her hand to gain her attention, and as she looked down, he continued to bounce. "It's a boy, so we thought of boy names. I thought of Brownie, 'cause he's all brown—"

"I thought of Chester, which is short for Chestnut since he's kind of the color of a chestnut," Lily pronounced.

"Oh, I see. Well, um…" She wasn't sure if she was expected to throw in an opinion, so she glanced between her kids and a smiling Ben, who just shook his head.

"But then he kept bounding around," Anna said with a laugh. "So, the kids decided on Bounder."

"Bounder?" As soon as she said the word, the dog

jumped up again, his tongue lolling to one side as he appeared to grin. "I guess Bounder it is!"

After another moment of everyone giving their attention to the new member of the family, she looked toward the kids and said, "Go ahead and get your backpack so we can go home. And make sure to thank Mrs. Popovich for letting you stay." The kids rushed over to the table, putting away the game and gathering their backpacks, eagerly accepting the plastic tub filled with cookies. Stepping over to Anna, she placed her hand on the older woman's arm. "I can't thank you enough for watching the kids tonight. I promise this won't happen again. I told my boss that I wasn't going to stay late anymore."

"Oh, my dear, your children are adorable. They're lovely to be with and we had such a good time. I know you worry about me, but I gain strength every day, and with Benjamin here, I promise we were all safe." Turning, Anna picked up another plastic container from the counter and handed it to Violet. "In case you didn't eat tonight, here's some dinner you can heat up."

After hugging the older woman, she stepped to the side so that the kids could offer Anna hugs, and then headed out on the deck, surprised when Ben followed.

"I'll walk you over," he said.

She didn't refuse, and soon the kids rushed through their back door. She watched as Lily placed the cookies onto the kitchen counter, and both kids dropped their backpacks in the dining room. Calling out their goodbyes to Ben, they ran into the living room to watch TV before bedtime. She and Ben stopped in the kitchen, and she turned to say goodbye to him as well, but he spoke before she had a chance.

He stepped closer and lowered his voice. "Violet, I need to apologize for coming over and going around your house earlier. The kids wanted to change clothes, and Babciu asked if I would come and make sure they were okay. As soon as we got here, they wanted to show me the bathrooms and what might need to be fixed. Then Charlie wanted to show me his room, and Lily wanted to show me hers. I should've said no. I was uncomfortable being in your house without you being here, and should have just said—"

"It's okay. Really." His hand was resting on her kitchen counter and she reached out, placing hers on top. As soon as their fingers touched, she felt a warm tingle and blinked in surprise. Sure that she must be the only one who felt that, she looked up but watched as his eyes opened wide, staring first at their hands before turning his gaze up toward her face. Not wanting to show her nervousness, she continued, "It's not like I have any secrets here in the house. But I appreciate you letting me know." She glanced toward the powder room and snorted. "I'm embarrassed, though, to think that you had to see all the warts my house has."

His thumb moved gently over her hand, and she fought to keep from curling her fingers into his. The pull was magnetic, and they leaned closer at the same time.

"All of these old townhouses have issues. Honestly, Violet, it looks like most of yours are cosmetic, although you might want to consider replacing some of your copper pipes with PVC, and that would help with rust stains. You also might want to consider replacing your windows."

Her nose scrunched as she nodded. "We discovered as soon as the wind began to blow that the cold would seep through the spaces around the windows."

They were now much closer, and she noticed his eyes had flecks of gold. He didn't seem as though he was in a hurry to leave, and she didn't want him to. His eyes were mesmerizing, but it was his lips that now held her attention. Strong but full. The kind of lips on a man that made a woman think about kissing. *What would he feel like? What would he taste like?* He leaned a little closer and his gaze focused on her lips as well, his pupils dilating. If she just lifted a little onto her toes—

He sucked in a quick breath and leaned back, keeping his hand connected to hers but moving his lips away. She felt the loss and hadn't even tasted him yet. *Yet? Would there be another chance?*

Finding her breath rushing from her lungs, she breathed, "Would you like something to drink?"

He glanced toward the counter where the plastic container rested near their hands. "You need to heat the dinner that my babcia sent over. I'll get out of your way."

"You're not in my way, Ben. I'll just heat it in the microwave, but I've got some wine or beer if you'd like."

He gave her hand a little squeeze, nodded, and smiled. "Beer would be good."

She felt his smile pierce inside and returned it with one of her own. Moving toward the refrigerator, she hated that the movement took her hand away from his. She retrieved a beer for him and a wine bottle. He reached out to take the wine bottle and glanced around, his gaze landing on a clean wine glass resting on the dryer rack next to the sink. He poured while she nuked the casserole Anna had sent over. She knew she should invite him to sit at the dining room table, but that would mean competing with the sound of the TV.

"You should get off your feet," he said, reaching out to tuck a wayward strand of hair behind her ear.

The simple gesture had such an intimate feel, and she wanted to turn her cheek into his palm. Instead, she turned and walked into the dining room, placing her plate and glass onto the table, and waited until he sat as well. The TV clicked off, and the sound of whispering came from the living room. Looking over her shoulder, she caught a glimpse of the kids climbing off the sofa.

"Mom, we're tired and going on up," Lily announced, running in to offer a hug.

"Oh... okay," she barely managed to get out before Charlie followed suit. As Charlie's arms surrounded her, she watched as Lily moved to Ben, offering him a hug as well. She was shocked when Charlie followed his sister's lead and hugged Ben, too.

"Ben?" Charlie began. "You'll keep Bounder, right? He'll be able to watch over the yard tonight to keep the bad men away?"

She caught Ben's gaze over Charlie's head, her concern palpable. Looking back down at Charlie, he nodded. "Yep. Bounder will stay in the house so he can watch over both our yards."

The little boy breathed a huge sigh of relief before turning and running up the stairs after Lily.

"Are you okay?" Ben asked, drawing her attention back to him.

"Well, the kids are never bad about bedtime, but for them to turn off the TV without being asked and get ready for bed without a bit of nagging is a surprise. And as far as Charlie goes, I'll have him wake me up when he has nightmares."

"It seems like having the dog around might help with that."

She nodded her agreement before spooning into her casserole. The explosion of flavors hit her tongue. "Oh, this is amazing. I was really hungry."

His brow furrowed. "You didn't have a chance to eat even though you worked late?"

She took a sip of wine and said, "Well, I could have, but let's just say that I didn't want to spend the money or *owe* my boss any favors."

He reared back in his chair, his gaze now narrowed. "What kind of favors?"

She waved her hand dismissively. "Just the same problem that many people have, especially women with a boss that doesn't like to be turned down."

"What the fuck—uh... heck, Violet?"

Licking her lips, she shrugged. "It's a small company. No HR. No managers. Just a boss who runs things the way he wants."

"Can you find another job?"

"Soon." Seeing his quizzical expression, she explained, "I'm almost finished with my degree. I have finals in another week, and then I can look for a new job."

"Was your boss always like that?"

"No. I was hired by his uncle right before Lily was born. He was a wonderful boss and took care of me. I was so lucky to have found a job with good insurance."

"And now?"

"Now, he's gone, and his nephew is the boss. He's expressed interest in me and has made my job mostly reception instead of bookkeeping. Unless, like tonight, he needs my help." She sighed heavily. "But within a few weeks, I should be able to put in for a better job."

"What are you looking for?"

She leaned back in her chair, loving the easy way she and Ben could converse. It had been a long time since someone took an interest in what she wanted. "I'd love to be an office manager as well as doing bookkeeping. I can still do bookkeeping but would like more managerial responsibilities."

"With a big company?"

"Only if I had to go with a larger company. I really like the idea of a smaller business where I can get to know the employees. Not be treated like a number." They were quiet for a moment as he sipped his beer and she finished her dinner. Looking up, she added, "I suppose you think I should tell my boss to go stuff himself and quit immediately."

Ben shook his head with vigor. "No, I don't. I hate like hell you have to deal with that boss, but I understand that finding a new job is tough."

"Having two kids, I need the insurance. That's the

only reason I've stuck it out so long. The benefits were necessary, especially after Matt died."

Silence filled the air around them.

"Can I ask how he died?" Ben's question was low, almost hesitant.

"Of course. It's no secret. He was in a car accident." The words came easily, practiced over the years, given to multiple acquaintances, even strangers who asked about her widow status. *A car accident.* She could say the three words with no bitter edge, allowing them to slip over her lips as though she was reciting the death of someone older where the cause wasn't questioned. Pushing her now-empty dish away, she turned back to him, blinking in surprise at the intense expression on his face as he leaned closer.

"I'm sure you've said those words so many times over the years, and I'm sorry. But the look on your face... why do I get the feeling that there's a lot more to the story?"

Her chest heaved and she swallowed audibly. "Oh... you're good at reading people."

"I had to be. My team often depended on it."

"Yes, well, I... uh..." She cleared her throat and tried to speak again but the words stuck in her throat.

"Mom?"

Charlie's call was a welcome respite from the intense gaze coming from Ben. Leaping to her feet, she looked down at him. "Sorry. I need to go up and see what he's into."

Ben stood and reached his hand out, giving hers a squeeze. "I'll let myself out and lock the door." He turned, then stopped and looked over his shoulder. "I'm sorry, Violet. I shouldn't have asked."

He was gone before she had a chance to call him back. Before she had a chance to assure him that his intuition was right. Before she had a chance to explain anything about her life and how much different it would be if Matt had not made the choices he did.

"Mom!"

Startling out of her reverie, she turned and hurried up the stairs.

11

Ben hopped over the fence, wincing as he tried to land on his good leg but still felt pain in his injured one. He stopped before he made it to his back door. He dropped his chin to his chest. *Fuck... I almost kissed Violet.* His heart raced with need and he adjusted his cock as it twitched at the thought of her lips. He tried to remember that she was a widow and a mother. Not to mention a woman who got hit on at work by a dick of a boss.

Blowing out a deep, cleansing breath in an attempt to gain control of his cock, he jogged onto the deck and through the sliding glass door, bolting it once he was inside.

"How was Violet?"

"Huh?" He jerked around, seeing his grandmother's smiling face. "Uh... what do you mean, how was Violet?"

She blinked in return. "What do you mean, what do I

mean? I was just wondering if she was all right from her long day?"

"Oh… right. She's fine. She liked the food you sent. The kids are fine, too. But then you knew that since they were here. But I mean they're fine… over at their house, too."

Her hands landed on her hips. "Benjamin Popovich, you're babbling, and you never babble. If I didn't know better, I'd think you were hiding something."

It was all he could do to keep from squirming under her perusal but shook his head, walking over to offer her a hug. "No, ma'am. I'm not hiding anything."

"Hmph." She leaned back and looked up into his face. "She's a very sweet woman."

"Yes, she is."

"And I would think any man would consider it an honor to ask her for a date."

Now it was his turn to hold her gaze. "I'm a former SEAL trying to figure out what's next in my life. I'm not sure that either of us is in the right place in our lives for a date right now."

"Hmph," she repeated, unknown thoughts playing behind her sharp eyes. "You know… people so often think that they have to have their lives all together before they're ready to be with someone. But I've always felt that it's the way two people can complement each other that makes for a better relationship. Sort of like missing pieces that come together… better together than alone."

She reached up and patted his cheek, and the

endearing touch was just as welcome as when he was younger.

"Well, I'm off to bed. I'll see you in the morning." She walked to the door of her room, much steadier as she barely leaned on her cane. Looking over her shoulder, she smiled. "If you ever want to ask her out, I'm more than happy to watch the children. They're very dear to me. And I think they'd love the idea." With that, she moved into her room, leaving him standing in the middle of the kitchen, wondering how he'd managed to lose control of his situation ever since he'd met the kids.

Looking down at Bounder who was sitting at his feet, tongue lolling, eyes staring up, he bent to rub the attention-eager dog's head. "I'm not sure I can handle more than being your dad right now, boy. But you've got a job... keep the bad men away from Charlie." Flipping off the lights, he patted the blanket on the floor, watched the dog curl up on it, and then headed upstairs.

He read in bed for a while but quickly abandoned his book. The memory of being so close to Violet stayed with him. Her curves demurely covered by professional slacks and a light pink blouse. The scent of her floral shampoo. Her dark hair pulled back with an elaborate clip, a few tendrils escaping their confinement and framing her oval face. Her deep blue-purple eyes staring up at him before dropping to his lips. He could swear that if he'd leaned closer, they would have kissed. And her lips would have tasted as sweet as he imagined. And he'd imagined her lips against his a lot.

A single mom trying to finish school and look for a

new job with a townhouse that needs serious upkeep. A former SEAL who just recently left the service with a bum knee and a grandmother who needs his help. *What the hell could we possibly do for each other besides tangle in the sheets?* Which he had no doubt would be phenomenal.

Sighing heavily, he thought of what his grandmother had said. *It's the way two people can complement each other that makes for a better relationship.* The night offered no answers, so he turned off his light and slid under the covers.

Hours later, he woke to the sound of snores. Looking next to the bed, he realized Bounder had crept upstairs and curled up on the rug. He started to get up and take the dog back downstairs, but the call of slumber was too great. Rolling over, he went back to sleep.

Later, he woke to the sound of distant whimpering. Looking around, Bounder was nowhere to be seen. Wanting to make sure his grandmother was okay, he leaped from the bed and hurried down the stairs. Darting through the kitchen, he spied Bounder standing at the sliding glass door, looking out into the dark yard, pawing at the door. "Hold on, buddy. I need to check on Babciu." Opening her door, he peered in and could see her asleep in bed, her chest rising and falling easily with her breathing. Tiptoeing back out, he padded into the kitchen, his gaze landing on the dog still whimpering at the door.

Flipping on the light at the door that illuminated the deck, he saw nothing. Opening the door, he let Bounder race outside to disappear into the corner of the dark yard. Violet's yard was also dark. Deciding outdoor security lighting was needed, he put that on his mental list.

A light went on in one of the upstairs bedrooms of Violet's house. *Charlie's room.* He wondered if he'd had nightmares again. Bounder was still sniffing the back fence, and he called him over. "Come on, boy."

The dog reluctantly came to Ben, circling the blanket in the kitchen several times before laying down. Deciding to leave the deck light on, he double-checked the locks and headed back upstairs. He assumed Bounder would follow, but the dog stayed downstairs.

Now wide-awake, Ben lay in bed, his mind turning over the idea of asking Violet for a date. *But does it make any sense?* It was one thing to have a quick fuck or even a fling that might last for several days during a leave when he was back in the states after having been overseas on a mission. But Violet would never just be a fuck or a fling. *So, what do I have to offer?* For a man who struggled with the idea of forever, he wasn't sure he had an answer to that question.

Ben hit the home store the next day, buying everything he needed to continue working on his babcia's house and to start a few projects on Violet's. Since it was Friday, he hadn't expected the store to have quite so many customers. He'd found everything he wanted but had to wait in a long line.

"Looks like you've got a busy weekend planned."

Hearing the words coming from behind him, he turned and looked at the man in line with a huge flatbed cart filled with supplies. The man was tall, slightly barrel-chested, with dark hair cut high and tight, shot with a bit of silver. His appearance screamed former military.

"Yes. Working on my grandmother's house to get it ready to sell when she decides she's ready." He tilted his head down to the man's cart. "You?"

"I own Anderson's Construction Services. I'm a local contractor, hiring veterans."

"I thought you were military."

Grinning, the man nodded. "Navy. Did fifteen years then got out to help my father with his construction business." He scanned Ben with an eagle-eye stare "And you?"

"Navy. SEAL. Just got out. Fifteen years also."

The man stuck his hand out, clasping Ben's in a firm grip. "I'm Daniel. Daniel Anderson."

"Ben Popovich." They moved up in line a few feet.

"So, Ben, tell me about your grandmother's place."

They killed time in line as Ben described the work he was doing, expounding on the renovations his grandfather had accomplished years prior. Daniel listened, nodded, and offered a few suggestions.

"You know, if you ever decide that you'd like to work for us, here's my card. I'm always looking for hardworking veterans to join Anderson Contracting. Even if you just work for a few years and get your own license, I'm good with that, too."

Taking the card, he felt a surge of energy jolt

through him, something he realized he'd been missing ever since he'd torn his knee up the last time. Wanting to be upfront, he said, "You should be warned that I've got a bum knee."

Daniel threw his head back and laughed. He pulled up his pants leg and Ben stared at a prosthetic leg. "Below the knee amputee."

"Damn," he breathed, admiration for Daniel ratcheting up.

Still smiling, Daniel said, "You won't find me climbing on the roofs of any of our houses, but just about everything else, I can do."

Moving to the cash register, he tucked Daniel's card into his pocket before paying for his purchases. After completing his transactions, he pushed his cart out of the way and turned back to Daniel. "Sir, it was good to meet you."

"Same to you, Ben. I wish you luck with your projects, and keep me in mind."

Reaching out to shake his hand, he nodded. "I will. I... well, I'll give you a call." With Daniel's well wishes ringing in his ear, he pushed his cart out to his SUV, his step—and his heart—lighter.

Once home, he unloaded his purchases and carried them to the back door, his footsteps accompanied by Bounder's enthusiastic presence. Letting both of them into the kitchen, he smiled at his grandmother stirring a pot on the stove. The scent of butter, cream cheese, chocolate, and almonds filled the air. Walking over, he bent and kissed her cheek. "Babciu, you're going to make me fat."

Laughing, she shook her head. "These are for the church meeting."

He cocked his eyebrow and placed his hand on his heart as though wounded. "All of them?"

"Most of them, although I suppose I might could set aside a few for you and the Mayfields." She turned back to the stove, stirring her concoction, her lips quirking upward. "What's on your agenda for today?"

He rubbed his chin and hesitated. He wasn't surprised when she twisted around and speared him with another stare. "I met someone at the home store. A man... a veteran who runs a construction company that hires veterans."

She laid the spoon onto the counter and turned to give him her full attention. He smiled, her actions so like he remembered when growing up. She had always given attention to him when he needed to talk, seeming to instinctively tell when he was lost, confused, worried, or just grieving.

Plunging in, he said, "I like working with my hands... always have. I'm good at taking things apart and putting them back together. I'm good at figuring out what needs to be done and coming up with a plan to accomplish that. I can work fast and methodically, depending on what needs to be done. These are all things I know grandpa did when he was redoing this house. I learned a lot from him and didn't even realize it at the time."

"Do you think that you'd like to be a contractor?"

He snorted as he shook his head. "It seems weird to

be thirty-three and trying to figure out what I want to be when I *grow up.*"

She chuckled as well. "Life is full of change, Benjamin. You may be grown up already but that doesn't mean that things are written in stone."

"That's for damn sure." He watched as she glanced down at the pot and stirred once more. "But yeah, I think I'd like to try it. I'm getting an idea of how things work by fixing your place and what I plan on doing for Violet's place. But I'm considering calling Daniel—uh, that's the contractor. Daniel Anderson."

"Hmmm, Anderson Contracting. I remember a Dylan Anderson who used to be in the construction business. Your grandfather did some work with him at one time."

"He said his father started the company."

"Well, well. Small world," she murmured, smiling. "So, when are you going to work on Violet's house?"

"I thought I'd work here today and then over at her house tomorrow since she and the kids will be home." He turned to walk out of the kitchen and looked down to see Bounder sleeping on his blanket. "That reminds me, did you hear anything in the backyard last night?"

She tilted her head to the side. "Hear anything? Like what?"

"I don't know. Bounder was whimpering but not barking. Then I let him out and he raced to the back fence, sniffing around. With neither of our bedrooms on the back of the house, I didn't figure you heard anything."

"I confess, I slept like a baby."

Grinning, glad that she was sleeping well, he added, "I bought motion sensor lights for the back. We should have better lighting at the back of the house anyway." With that, he headed outside to begin his work for the day. Glancing toward Violet's house, he found that he looked forward to Charlie and Lily getting home from school.

12

"So, how does it work?"

Ben looked down from the ladder he was on and smiled toward Charlie, who was holding the lamp in his hands. "It has electronic eyes that detect something called infrared waves. Those are heat waves, and they radiate from moving objects. When it detects those waves, it triggers the light to turn on."

Charlie seemed to ponder the explanation, then asked, "Any moving object?" Ben nodded and Charlie continued. "What if there's someone walking on the sidewalk?"

"We can set it for a range. Since I don't want it to go off every time somebody walks on the sidewalk, I'll have it angled more toward the yard."

"What if a cat jumps over the fence to get into the garbage can? Mom gets real mad when something gets into the garbage and makes a mess."

Ben chuckled and nodded. "Yeah, that can be a problem. It can also be a problem if the light keeps coming on and glares toward a neighbor's house. I'm going to try to set them so that they're angled at our backyards only."

Charlie looked at his backyard, then lifted his gaze toward Anna's double-wide yard, then turned toward the neighbor. "Even though our backyards meet up together, yours is a lot wider since your grandmother has two houses put together."

"You're a smart little boy, Charlie. I figure if the light goes on in your backyard, it will only shine toward us and neither my babcia nor I have bedrooms on the back, so it won't bother us. I admit that if they go off in our backyard, you might see the lights in your room since it's on the back of the house."

Charlie swung his head upward and scrunched his nose. "How'd you know that?"

"I was up there, remember?"

"Oh, yeah!"

He reached for the lamp and took it from Charlie's outstretched hands, who then took the old, inefficient lamp they were replacing.

"I can see there's no sensor on this one," Charlie said, turning it over in his hands. "What are you going to do with it?"

"Just throw it away."

"Can we take it apart first? I'd like to see what's on the inside."

Chuckling, Ben nodded. "I used to do that all the time, too. Take things apart and see how they work."

Charlie looked up, his eyes bright and his smile

wide. "I like you being over here, Ben. Sometimes, it's hard being the only guy."

Ben swallowed deeply, emotion rising to the surface as he thought of the meaning behind Charlie's words. *I like having a man around. I don't remember my dad. I feel lonely sometimes with just Mom and my sister.* Seeing Charlie still staring up at him, he forced a smile to his lips. "I like being here, too."

Turning back to the task, he held the new lamp in place with one hand and screwed in the bolts to affix it to the back of the house with the other. Movement caught his eye, and he spied Violet watching from the window over the kitchen sink. Her gaze was resting on Charlie, her smile soft. As her eyes lifted and met his, her smile widened. Grinning in return, he quickly tightened the bolts, then climbed down off the ladder.

Lily bounded outside with Violet and looked up at the lamp. Before she had a chance to ask, Charlie stated, "It's got an in-fa-red detector. It can see motion and then turn the light on."

"Good, Charlie," Ben said, his hand landing on the little boy's shoulder.

Violet exclaimed, "My goodness! I was going to make sure you weren't in Ben's way, but it sounds like you're learning a lot."

"Oh, Mom, I'm not in the way," Charlie groused. "I'm helping, right, Ben?"

"That's right, you are."

"Well, can I entice you two in for lunch? Lily and I made tacos."

Charlie threw his hands into the air and shouted his

approval of the menu. Laughing, Ben nodded. "I guess that means we eat tacos." Looking down, he said, "Make sure to wash up since we've been working out here."

Charlie ran inside and Violet's brows lifted to her forehead. "Wow... you got him to wash up without pleading or bribing!"

"It's a bro-code," Lily said, rolling her eyes.

Ben looked at her in surprise, and from Violet's wide eyes, he felt her surprise as well.

"Bro-code? Where on earth did you hear that?" Violet asked, her hands landing on her hips as she stared down at her daughter.

"Oh, Mom, it's nothing bad. It just means that it's the way men talk to each other. Kind of like they have their own secret language." Lily giggled and followed her brother inside.

Violet's gaze met his and she shook her head. "Sometimes Lily sounds like a miniature teenager and other times like a little girl. I never know what's going to come out of her mouth!"

Picking up his tools and setting the ladder over to the side, he admitted, "Gotta tell you, women have always been somewhat of a mystery to me, and it doesn't seem to matter the age."

Violet stepped closer, her hand resting gently on his arm. "And me? Am I a mystery?"

The feel of her fingers on his bare arm sent a warm tingle over his skin. Unable to take his eyes off her face, he stepped closer. "You, beautiful lady, are a huge mystery."

She blushed and shook her head. "Thank you... but

I'm really not a mystery. Pretty much, what you see is all there is."

Desire filled him at the thought that he liked what he saw. He leaned closer—

"Mom! Lily says I can't have three tacos!"

She backed away, regret mixed with desire now in her eyes. "Sorry," she whispered, then headed inside.

Ben stayed outside for another moment, willing his cock to behave. Once he was sure he could enter the house without his cock leading the way, he followed the others.

Lunch was fun and the conversation lively. Laughing freely at the antics of Charlie and Lily, he listened to their stories and paid close attention to the loving way Violet encouraged their imagination while making sure each child ate well and behaved. His grandparents had been wonderful to him, but now he realized how much he missed out on not having siblings.

"What are you going to do this afternoon, Ben?"

"Well," he began, turning his attention to Lily. Her dark hair was pulled back in a ponytail, and with her blue eyes pinned on him, it hit him how much she looked like her mother. "Um... I thought I would fix the leaky faucet in the downstairs bathroom. I also bought a special cleanser just for old rust stains and a sink chip-fixer."

"Chip-fixer?"

He nodded. "Yeah... think of it like your dentist filling a tooth that had a cavity. Same kind of idea. Then I'll need to measure the windows that need to be replaced."

"Can I help with that?" Lily asked.

Before he could answer, Violet said, "Kids, Ben might not need someone underfoot."

"No," he assured. "They're fine." She smiled her thanks and, gut-punched, he smiled back.

A few hours later, he and Lily had measured the windows, and she had carefully written down the dimensions on a pad of paper, labeling each window with the correct room. Standing in her room, he nodded toward the boy-band poster. "They any good?"

She scrunched her nose and shook her head. "Not really, but the one in the middle is cute, isn't he?"

"Not sure I'm qualified to judge what's cute."

She stared for a moment then said, "Well, do you think my mom is cute?"

The end of the tape measure slipped from his hand, snapping back into its holder with a *zip*. "Uh... yeah... sure. I mean, yes, your mom is very... uh... pretty."

"Yeah, I think so, too."

He held his breath, wondering what else she was going to say, but she looked down at her pad of paper and continued to write. Swallowing audibly, he remeasured the window, having completely forgotten the last number. Calling it out, he watched as she wrote it down carefully.

She stood and handed the pad to him. "There, I think we got it." She looked around, her gaze not landing on anything in particular before she finally said, "I'm going to go see if Charlie wants to go over to your grandmother's house. I think she said she was baking today."

Without giving him a chance to reply, she darted out of the room and down the stairs. He walked into the hall and heard her say, "Mom, Charlie and I are going over to Mrs. Popovich's house. Ben said that she was expecting us to come over for cookies. We can see if there is anything we can help her with since Ben is over here."

"Oh... okay. Well, if Ben said she's expecting you, then it's fine," Violet said.

His brow furrowed as he wondered why Lily had lied, but then he knew Babciu would love the company. He heard the back door open and glanced out the window to see the kids running through the yard and clambering over the fence, much to the delight of Bounder. They raced to his back deck and she opened the sliding glass door, greeting the kids with hugs.

"Hey."

The soft voice from the doorway caused him to swing his head around and see Violet watching him. Smiling, he replied, "Hey, yourself."

She stepped into the room and looked around. He could have sworn her gaze landed on the photograph of Lily and her father on the nightstand before her focus moved back to him. "I hope the kids didn't bother you too much today."

He stepped closer, his vision filled with nothing but her. "They're no bother. They're great kids. Smart. Inquisitive."

She nodded, her gaze dropping to his lips, and she swallowed. "They went to Anna's for cookies."

Drawn by a magnetic force stronger than his will, he

stepped closer until her head leaned back to hold his gaze. Lifting a hand, he cupped her cheek. "So, we're alone."

"Yes," she breathed.

"I want to kiss you."

"Yes," she repeated, her voice barely above a whisper as her eyes dropped to his lips again.

Without fear of interruption, he bent and slowly kissed her, his lips molding to hers, the heat building in a slow burn. Just as he knew it would, she tasted of wild fruit and the scent of flowers from her shampoo filled his nostrils. Her lips were soft, and as she sighed, he slid his tongue inside, sweeping over hers.

His cock pressed against her soft belly, cradled as though they fit together perfectly. One arm banded around her waist, pulling her tighter, while the other continued to cup her cheek. The skin underneath his fingers was so soft, so delicate. Angling his head, he dove deeper, and her tongue tangled with his, sending jolts of electricity throughout his entire body. Wanting more of her soft skin, he slid his fingers underneath the bottom of her shirt, soothing his rough fingertips over her back.

Like a man who'd wandered the desert, he drank her in. All of his senses were firing... and misfiring. Unlike on a mission where he could separate his senses to keep absolute focus on the task, kissing Violet meshed the feel of her skin, her breasts crushed against his chest, scents, tastes, and sounds. Time ceased to exist. It didn't matter that they were standing in her daughter's bedroom with boy band posters staring at them from the wall. All that mattered was the woman in his arms, giving as much as she was receiving.

Kissing wasn't something he'd spent a lot of time doing, especially when the act of sex was just physical. While it might seem crazy, kissing was much more intimate than fucking.

But with Violet's body pressed from chest to knee against his, the petal-soft skin underneath his fingertips, her lips moving over his, and her tongue devouring his mouth, he experienced for the first time in his life a *kiss*. An all-involving, senses-firing, emotion-exploding kiss.

The sound of laughter from the backyard crept into his consciousness, and he dragged his lips away from hers, sucking in oxygen. Breathing heavily, he felt as though he were back in boot camp at the age of eighteen having run his first ten miles in full pack. Staring down into her beautiful eyes that were hooded with lust, he smiled and touched his lips to the tip of her nose. "I never wanted that kiss to end," he confessed.

She blinked several times as though trying to bring him back into focus before her lips curved upward. During the kiss her hands had crept to his shoulders, her fingers holding him tight. Now, her hands glided down, resting flat against his chest, and he had no doubt she could feel his pounding heartbeat.

"I didn't want it to end, either."

Not sure when the kids were going to return, he forced his legs to step back, immediately hating the cool air that moved between them but knowing his cock was straining against his jeans. Their heavy breaths continued for a moment as their gazes stayed locked.

Finally, they stepped completely apart just as they could hear the back door open.

"What are we doing?" she asked.

He watched as doubt and fear started to move into her eyes, and quickly said, "We're going to take the kids to dinner."

She blinked at his response before a small giggle slipped out. "Okay."

"Do the kids like pizza?"

"Do you know any kids that don't like pizza?"

Now it was his time to chuckle. "Honestly? I don't know a lot of kids. There was one back in California that I got to know, and yeah, he liked pizza."

"Then pizza it is," she agreed with a smile.

The kids came bounding up the stairs and ran into the room before they skidded to a halt. "Are y'all still here?" Charlie asked, his nose scrunching.

Ben noticed that Lily said nothing but stared between her mother and him, a slow smile playing about her lips.

Violet herded the children out of the room, asking about Anna, and telling them that they were going to get pizza that evening. Shouts and cheers met his ears, and he laughed as he followed them down the stairs.

13

Violet watched as her children ran around Pirate Ship Pizza, playing games while they waited for the pizza to arrive. They didn't come often, but the kids loved the chaotic atmosphere even though in her opinion the pizza was mediocre at best, and the wandering pirate mascot was scary. It had not escaped her attention that when they sat at the table, Lily steered Charlie to sit with her on one side, leaving Violet and Ben sitting next to each other. Now, she glanced to the side toward Ben, unable to hide her grin as his eyes darted in all directions. "Are you okay?"

He jerked his head around toward her, his eyes wide. "How the hell do you keep up with everything here? I keep trying to keep an eye on the kids, and it's impossible. It's loud, it's noisy, kids are running all over the place, lights are blinking, and that fuckin' scary-looking pirate looks more like a murderer out of a crappy movie than a children's mascot."

She barked out laughter, his expression as comical as his comments. "Oh, my God, Ben. That's hilarious. And you're so right!" It took her a moment to control her mirth, then she placed her hand on his arm and offered a consoling pat. "We used to come more often when we lived in a neighborhood not too far from here. We rarely make it now, so it's a treat for the kids. By the time we pay for the overpriced pizza, huge sugar-filled sodas, and buy the tokens so the kids can play all the games, it's not a cheap night out."

He placed his hand over hers that was still resting on his arm and squeezed. "This is my treat, so don't worry about the cost. Those kids did a great job helping me today, so I'm glad to give them what they want. Plus, I've eaten plenty of crappy food in my life, so greasy, cheesy pizza won't be a hardship. I just want to keep my eyes on the kids, but it's almost impossible."

"I know, and I worry too. That's why you heard me repeat the instructions that the kids have heard all their lives. Stay where they can see me. Don't go to the bathroom without letting me know. And never, ever leave with anyone, no matter what they're told."

"Good!"

She glanced down and sighed, nibbling on the corner of her mouth. Another squeeze on her hand brought her attention back up to Ben. Tilting her head slightly, she waited to see what he was going to say.

"You look worried, Violet. Do you want me to go round up the kids?"

She shook her head. "No, the pizza will be here soon

and they'll come over. It's just… sometimes I wonder if I give too many warnings. If I scare the children with my rules and concerns."

"Hey," he said, using his free hand to place his knuckle under her chin and lifting her head slightly so that her gaze was once again on him. "You are a fantastic mom. And, Violet, it's a scary world out there. You have to make sure your kids are safe and know how to stay as safe as they can."

"They already know about loss… I just hate making them know that more bad things can happen." She watched him open his mouth, then hesitate and close it again. Curious, she prodded, "What are you thinking?"

"I… well, Charlie mentioned that nothing was forever the other day. And I just wondered… well… their dad… I saw the pictures… shit, I'm not saying this very well."

Her heart warmed at his obvious concern but also the nervous way he tried to broach a difficult subject. A server walked toward the table, her arm loaded with a huge pan of pizza. Patting his arm again, she said, "It's time to eat. But if you can make it through a Pirate Pizza dinner with my kids, then we can talk later."

He leaned forward with a grin on his face, and she wondered if he was going to kiss her in the middle of the restaurant. Instead, he tucked a wayward tendril of hair behind her ear.

"It's a deal," he whispered, and his warm breath coasted over her cheek.

Before she could gain her wits, Lily and Charlie

raced over, another little girl with them. "Mom! We found Colleen!"

Violet smiled at Lily's friend, then her smile widened as she looked up to see Colleen's mom and dad walking toward them. Standing, she greeted them, drawing the other woman in for a hug. "Tara, it's so good to see you." She had only met Tara's handsome new husband a few times but loved the way he'd adopted Colleen as his own.

"Ben, this is my good friend, Tara... um... Fiske."

Ben shook her hand as Violet shook her head. "I'm sorry, I stumbled over your married name." Turning back to Ben, she explained, "Tara and I met several years ago when we lived near them. Her daughter went to the same school as Lily, and they used to wait at the bus stop together. And this is her husband, Carter. He's a... policeman?" She blushed at her inadequate introduction skills. "I'm so sorry, I should know this."

"He's my daddy now!" Colleen announced, grinning as she stared up at him as though he hung the moon and stars for her.

Carter, a tall, reddish-blonde man with an easy smile, stepped forward. "It's good to see you again, Violet, and don't worry about the introductions." He turned to Ben and the two men shook hands. "I'm a detective for the Hope City Police Department."

"This is Ben Popovich. He's... um... lives behind us." Chuckling, Ben placed his hand on Violet's back, his touch grounding her as she floundered.

"I'm recently out of the military and helping my grandmother with her house."

"And he's showing me how to fix houses!" Charlie piped up, climbing up on a chair to get closer to Ben.

Tara's eyes twinkled. "Hmm, just a helpful neighbor?"

Carter snagged Colleen before she mimicked Charlie and climbed onto a chair. His other arm slid around Tara's waist.

Violet felt her face heat while making big eyes at her friend. Ben's attention had already snapped to Charlie, holding him steady while whispering, "Gotta sit in the chair, not stand, buddy." Looking up again, he smiled at the other couple. "Would you like to join us? Our pizza is just here, and we can share then order more."

Violet's heart warmed again at the sight of Ben managing Charlie in a calm way while greeting her friends and accepting them to share their evening. She caught Tara's bright smile and wink, letting her know her friend approved.

"Thanks so much, but we've eaten and were just on our way out." The two women hugged and Tara whispered, "Call me. I want the scoop!" Before Violet had a chance to react, Tara turned toward Ben. "I hope we have a chance to see you again. Perhaps the kids can have a playdate soon."

"I'd like that," he said easily, shaking Carter's hand once more. As the Fiskes walked out of the restaurant, Charlie and Lily plopped into their seats, clapping as the pizza was placed in the middle of their table and four smaller plates were set next to it.

Serving the kids first, she sat down to see that Ben had placed pizza on her plate. Such a tiny gesture, but it was nice to have someone take care of her for a change. She had to remind the kids to not talk and eat at the same time, and they all dug into the pizza.

"Mom, guess who else I saw?" Lily asked, taking a big gulp of her drink. She began rattling off the names of some friends, soon to be challenged for airtime by Charlie, who wanted to tell what he'd been doing as well.

Looking over at Ben, she grinned and shook her head. "You can now see why I suggested we wait until later to talk."

He chuckled before turning his attention back to the kids, asking them questions and nodding at their replies. It didn't miss her notice how desperately they were soaking up his attention. Blinking away the gathering moisture, she smiled at their antics while making sure they ate.

"Ben, can you take me to the restroom?" Charlie asked, wiping his hands on the napkin.

Violet blinked in surprise. "Honey, you can just go with Lily and me—"

"I've got him," Ben said.

She swung her head between the two, seeing Ben's easy smile and wink and her son's relief visible in his wide smile, and her heart squeezed in her chest.

"We guys have to stick together, don't we?" Ben continued.

"Yes!" Charlie exuded, jumping to his feet. "I hate going to the ladies' bathroom, but Mom won't let me go into the boy's room by myself yet."

Ben nodded, pushing his chair back to stand. "Well,

that's because she cares about you. But if I'm around, you can go with me."

As the two males headed toward the men's room, she couldn't take her eyes off them. Ben's head was inclined toward Charlie, listening as the little boy talked nonstop. And Ben looked scrumptious in the jeans that fit his ass and thighs and in the front cupped part of him that had filled a few late-night fantasies.

"I really liked helping Ben today."

Turning toward Lily, she nodded. When serious, her daughter looked so much like her, and Violet once again wished her children could have had a carefree child-hood. "I'm glad, sweetie."

"He let us help and didn't treat us like we couldn't do anything."

Recognizing her daughter seemed to have a point to make, she nodded but remained quiet.

Lily wiped her hands and took another sip of her soda before lifting her gaze back to her mom. "Do you like Ben?"

"Of course. He's a good neighbor and easy to like," she replied, choosing her words carefully.

"No, I mean do you *like* him," Lily prodded, her fingers making air quotes at the word 'like'.

Sucking in her lips, she hesitated, not having a clue how to approach her response. "Lily, honey, right now I'm focusing on being a good mom to you and your brother, being a good student so I can get a better job, and being a good neighbor to Anna and Ben. So, that pretty much takes up my time."

"Yeah, but I know other kids whose parents got

divorced and they date. Colleen's last name is now her stepdad's name. Patty has a stepdad and a stepmom. Rick has had two stepdads, which I think is weird, but he says his mom just likes being married. Something about her not wanting to be a single mom. And my teacher got divorced and she's already dating someone."

Violet jerked slightly at hearing her nine-year-old daughter explain adult dating. "It's not quite the same for me—"

"Because Dad died?"

Blowing out a breath, she nodded slowly. "Yes... maybe... no. To be honest, I'm not sure. But, I don't want to jump into dating unless I meet someone special."

"Like Ben."

Her gaze snagged on Ben and Charlie walking back toward the table, Charlie just as animated as when they left. Her lips curved slightly at the sight of the two of them together.

"Never mind, Mom. I can see it on your face."

"Wh... what?" she asked, feeling a deep heat rise from her chest upward, knowing a tale-tell blush was evident. "I was just watching Charlie." Pinning Lily with a lifted-eyebrow stare, she said, "And stop trying to play matchmaker, young lady. I'm just fine as I am."

Something flashed through Lily's eyes, something undefinable, and Violet's chest squeezed again. The same daughter who was playing games earlier now seemed so grown up. Before she had a chance to blink, Lily turned to Charlie, grinned widely, and said, "Come on, let's get some more games in before we have to leave!"

Ben sat down, concern on his face. "Hey, are you okay? Everything okay with Lily?"

"Yes, absolutely. We were just chatting, that's all." Holding his gaze, she stared into his eyes, wondering what Lily observed when Violet looked at Ben... and hoped that she hid it from him. *The last thing he needs is some clinging woman thinking a kiss is more than it is.* Clearing her throat, she asked, "I saw Charlie talking your ear off. Anything I should know about?"

Chuckling, Ben shook his head. "Nah... he replayed all the games he won and fussed about the ones that were too hard. Honestly, those were only the ones where he was supposed to toss the ball into the holes. I told him that whenever he wanted, I could help him practice pitches in the backyard, and then when we came back here, he'd be ready."

She kept a smile plastered on her face, not wanting to scare Ben by bursting into tears. But he could have no idea what his words would have meant to Charlie— or her. Somehow, she managed to croak out a 'Thank you'. His eyes searched her face, but she kept her smile intact.

He leaned closer, and this time placed a soft kiss on her cheek, right at the corner of her mouth. It was over quickly but melted her heart.

Several hours later, she opened the back door and welcomed him into the kitchen. When they had returned home from Pirate Pizza, Ben went back to

Anna's house to check on her while she made sure the kids were bathed and ready for bed. Charlie and Lily's earlier excitement had morphed into exhaustion, and the kids were now tucked into bed, sound asleep.

"Hey, come on in," she invited, leading him into the house. "I've got a beer for you and poured some wine for me."

He kissed her lightly, then grabbed the beer and followed her into the living room. She settled on one end of the sofa, her body twisting toward him as he sat in the middle.

"Are the kids in bed?"

Laughing softly, she nodded. "Oh, yeah. They took a bath, brushed their teeth, and put on their jammies. Then fell into their beds and were o-u-t out." She sipped her wine before replacing the glass on the coffee table. "I want to thank you for tonight. They had such a good time."

"I did, too. I told Babciu that I hadn't had that much fun in a long time."

She smiled, warmed that he enjoyed spending time with her kids as well as her.

"Your friends seemed nice."

"Tara? Yes, she's a dear. We met years ago dropping the kids off at school and just clicked. She's a social worker and maybe that's why she's so easy to talk to. She never met Matt, so she's only known me as a widow. She grew up in Hope City, has a huge family, and they all still live nearby. I always envied her that support system. Her first husband was a loser, and she's raised Colleen practically by herself... well, until Carter came along." Having mentioned Matt's name, she sighed, knowing it was time. "You wondered about their father…"

His body was twisted toward hers and his arm was draped over the back of the sofa, his fingertips rubbing her shoulder. "Yeah… whatever you'd like to tell me."

"I'll talk softly, but I should let you know that I've made sure their doors are closed. There are some things they know about Matt and other things that I've kept from them." Sighing again, she said, "But I feel like I want to explain things in more depth to you."

"I'd like that, Violet."

"Matt and I met in high school and started dating when he was a senior and I was a sophomore. Since he went to Hope City University, we kept dating, and after I graduated, I started there as well. When he graduated, he wanted to get married, and I was young, in love, and foolish. Instead of waiting, I dropped out of college, and thinking I was so grown up, we got married. I started working and a year later we had Lily. I felt as though I had the perfect life. A husband I loved and a child born of that love. A job I enjoyed. And several years later, I had Charlie. Matt was a good husband and a good father. My life seemed almost perfect. I never imagined how it would change."

She thought talking about Matt would be uncomfortable, dredging up memories she'd rather leave behind. But with Ben's soothing touch, warmth spread through her, and for the first time in a long time, she didn't feel so alone.

"Things began to change, but I didn't notice it at the

time... it was only in retrospect that I realized it. My focus was on raising the kids, keeping the house, and my job. I was a bookkeeper, and my boss let me cut my hours back to part-time. Matt got a promotion and was spending more time at the office. He seemed happy, and I was happy for him." She lifted her hand and gently rubbed her forehead, casting her mind back. "There were little signs that things were changing, but I couldn't imagine any young family like ours not having to deal with certain issues. There were a few times that he would come home from work and I smelled alcohol. Not a lot. He certainly didn't reek and didn't appear inebriated. When I asked about it, he said that some coworkers occasionally went to bars after work, and said it was needed for networking." Snorting, she shook her head. "What did I know of the corporate world? I had complete faith and trust in my husband. Other than that, I thought things were fine. He was good with the kids and we had a lot of fun on weekends. Our sex life was good, or at least I thought it was. But there was the night of the accident."

She glanced beyond Ben toward the stairs, listening to make sure she didn't hear the children.

"Do you want to go check to see if their doors are still closed?" he whispered.

Loving that he understood her feelings, she nodded. She stood and tiptoed halfway up the stairs until she could see that Charlie and Lily's doors were shut. Descending, she moved straight to the sofa and sat. "Thanks for that."

"It's all good, Violet. What you're telling me takes a good deal of strength and focus. I want to make it as easy on you as possible, and that includes making sure Charlie and Lily are protected."

Her eyes closed slowly as his words settled deep inside, filling a place that had been dug out and empty ever since Matt had died. Sucking in a ragged breath, she refocused on the feel of Ben's fingers gently massaging her shoulder, bringing her back to the here and now where her emotions were safe. Opening her eyes, she continued.

"Matt didn't come home one evening, and I was worried. It was much later than he'd ever been out. The kids had already been put to bed, and I sat for several hours just waiting on him. He didn't answer his phone or texts. I tried calling a couple of his coworkers that were buddies, but while they admitted he'd been out having drinks with them, he'd already left. And then there was the knock on the door."

She took another sip of wine, hoping not to slosh it over the rim considering her fingers were shaking. "I knew before I opened the door that it was the police. And yet when I saw them, it was all I could do to lock my knees in place so that I didn't drop to the floor. They told me Matt had been killed in a car accident."

"Violet, I'm so sorry."

She'd heard those words so often over the years, and her response was always to smile politely and thank the other person. But this time, with Ben, she wanted to push on with her story. She wanted to tell him what very few people knew other than her parents, Matt's parents, and a few close friends.

"He wasn't alone in the car."

Ben's eyes widened as understanding appeared to dawn, and his mouth dropped open. "Fuckin' hell."

14

_____

"Fuckin' hell." The words erupted from deep inside, slipping past his lips before he had a chance to hold them back.

She shook her head slowly. "Yep. That's what I say, too."

"How did you find out?" He winced at his question, but she seemed to want to talk, and he wanted to give her that chance.

"It was at the visitation after the funeral. I overheard his friends talking."

Air rushed from his lungs, and now it was his time to shake his head in disbelief. At first, his fingers had halted at the shock of her words, but he continued to move his hand over her shoulder, hoping to warm her cool skin and ease the tension he felt underneath his fingertips.

"We had it at Matt's parents' house because I just didn't think I could handle having a lot of people in our house. Many guests had already left, and my parents were sitting with his parents in the living room while Charlie and Lily were taking a nap in an upstairs bedroom. I walked into the kitchen to get a drink of water and saw a group of Matt's friends just outside the kitchen window on the back deck. They had no idea the window was open."

She finished the last of her wine and placed the glass onto the coffee table. When she settled back onto the sofa, she was closer, her bent knee resting on his thigh.

"A friend of ours who'd taken a job out of town had come back for the funeral. He was standing out with the others, and they were catching him up on what had happened. From their account, Matt had been having an affair with a woman in the office for a couple of years. Supposedly, he was going to ask for a divorce, and then I got pregnant with Charlie and he told the other woman that while he wanted to be with her, he didn't want to be the kind of man who walked out on his pregnant wife." Violet snorted, then slapped her hand over her nose and mouth.

"That probably sounded ridiculous. It's just... I stood at the kitchen window and listened to these men talk about how great Matt was to not leave his pregnant wife when he was having an affair during that time."

"I'm sorry. I swear, Violet, I wish I could think of something else to say, but I'm speechless. I know people have affairs. I know people get divorced. But, Jesus, I'm just reeling from hearing what you had to go through."

He felt her shoulder lift in a small shrug but knew she was not unaffected by the events she was relating. He hoped she could feel his care through his touch.

"They continued to talk, so I pretty much got the whole story standing at the kitchen sink. The woman he was involved with was angry, but he supposedly continued to promise that he'd leave me. From my perspective, after Charlie was born, he was so in love with his son and very attentive to me. But looking back with this new information, his evenings out continued, so I guess his wife and family weren't enough to hold his full interest. Anyway, that evening, they'd been out drinking with these friends and had left. He was going to drop her off at her home, do whatever they did when they had a little bit of time, and then come home. But they never made it. No one else was involved in the accident. He simply took a curve too fast and slammed into a wall. I had already been told that his blood-alcohol level was above the legal limit, and, it seems, so was hers. They were both killed, so he not only took his life in the accident but hers as well."

In his mind he could see Violet standing at the kitchen window, her fingers tightly gripping the edge of the sink as she stared out at this group of men discussing her deceased husband. While he could imagine the scene, he couldn't imagine the pain she must have felt that day. Now, he understood why there were no pictures of her and Matt around the house, knowing that he'd been having an affair and had talked of leaving her and the kids. Thinking of the pictures of Matt and the kids that were placed in Charlie and Lily's rooms, he realized once again what a wonderful mother she was. Not willing to taint their memories and idea of their father, she wanted them to remember that he'd cared for them.

"What happened after you heard them talking?"

The corners of her lips turned down. "One of them turned around and saw me standing there and cursed. The others jerked around to see what he was looking at and saw me. No one moved. They stood and stared at me, and I stood and stared at them. Finally, the friend that had not known any of this came inside while the others left through the garden gate. He held me for a moment and swore he didn't know about what Matt had been doing. He left after a few minutes, and I walked into the living room. I'm embarrassed to say that I burst into tears and began babbling about what I heard. My parents were so upset, and then I realized Matt's parents hadn't said anything. I could tell by their expressions they knew."

"Dammit, Violet. Just when I think your story couldn't get worse, it does."

"I think his dad had seen Matt and this other woman out one time. Matt had assured his parents that it was over, but when she was killed in the car crash, they knew." She shrugged again and added, "I rarely see them now. I would never keep the children away from them, but they moved to Florida to be closer to their daughter. They send cards, and I know they love Lily and Charlie. I think they just don't know how to act. And that's fine with me. I know it's not their fault, but it was so painful to be in their presence as a big reminder of his infidelity."

They fell quiet, and Ben struggled with his emotions.

Violet slumped deeper into the sofa cushions near him, as though the telling of her story had wiped away the last vestiges of energy. Her eyes closed, whether in exhaustion or wanting to avoid looking at him, he didn't know. But for a moment, he was glad, simply because he wanted to say the right thing, do the right thing, but had no idea what that was.

This woman was strong, hard-working, beautiful, giving, loving... everything a man could want. Ben had witnessed infidelity but always at a distance. Over the years in the military, he'd seen friends receive Dear John letters where their spouses had found someone who'd be home and not on a mission. He'd also witnessed married comrades pick up women in bars when they were away from home. But he knew deep down in his core that could never be him. His parents' marriage had been strong from what he witnessed as a child and from what his grandparents told him. Certainly, his grandparents' marriage was long and loving. And with his SEAL team, those who found love remained faithful, loving, and dedicated.

"He was weak." He winced as his words slipped out unheeded before he had a chance to think them through. Violet's eyes jerked open, and she stared at him. Deciding he'd already stepped into the situation, he continued. "He was a weak man. A weak husband. A weak father. Just fuckin' weak."

She licked her lips and nodded slowly. "I know, and I agree. Believe me, I went through all the emotions you'd imagine. Shock. Disbelief. Hurt. Anger. A lot of anger. It was hard not to internalize it all. Why? Wasn't I good enough? Weren't we enough for him? What could I have done?"

"Nothing. There was nothing you could have done because he was the weak link." He watched her tilt her head to the side in silent question. He pulled his thoughts together, praying he could help her understand what he was thinking. "As SEALs, we're not allowed a weak link. We succeed because everyone on the team is the best we can be. We had different specialties, but we were all fuckin' strong links in our chain. We had to go into missions knowing that every single one of us was strong enough to take care of anything that came along. To not be so could mean death for us all."

"Oh, Ben, I never thought about your former job. Or how it describes you... or maybe how you describe it."

He cupped her cheek, loving the feel of her soft skin. "I know I've never been married—hell, never been in a long-term relationship—but I know that both parties have to be strong. They can complement each other and work together to become stronger. But they both have to be strong. It can't be one strong and the other a weak link or the chain won't hold. Violet, it wasn't you. It was all on him. He was the weak link."

He had no idea if his words made sense but held his breath as she sucked in her lips, thoughts working behind her eyes. She nodded slowly, blowing out a heavy sigh.

"You're right. I never thought of it that way, but you're right."

"I can only imagine your pain and heartache. To deal

with the grief of death on top of the grief of infidelity would have taken a weaker person down. But that's not you. You're strong. You're resilient. And that's what you pass on to Lily and Charlie."

"I admit, it was hard. I told a few girlfriends. Tara knows. At least I had a small support system. But for the most part, the world expected a grieving widow... and I was... just grieving more than his death." With her last words, she grabbed his arm, her eyes wide as though pleading for him to understand. "I ached for the loss of my husband no matter the circumstances. I was lonely. I grieved for the loss of my children's father. All the things he would miss in their lives. Once I managed to make it past the anger, I thought that even if he had left us, he would still have been their father. Now, they have to go through life with no dad."

"I understand... at least part of that, I mean." He gently pulled her close and she shifted her body so that her head was tucked under his chin and her face was pressed against his chest. They sat as the clock ticked the minutes, both giving and taking comfort as they held each other. She felt so right in his arms, and he closed his eyes, allowing his senses to fill with her. Her breath puffed across his arm. Her heart beat in time with his. Her scent filled his nostrils. Her soft curves molded to the hard planes of his body. Everything about her called to him as no other woman ever had.

With his lips pressed to the top of her head, he whispered, "My parents were killed when I was ten years old. Grandpa and Babciu raised me." He felt her jerk but kept his arms around her. "It was a car accident, too. My grandparents swooped in and took care of everything. The funeral. Getting my things to their house, then taking care of my parents' house. Making sure I had what I needed. Christ, as hard as it was to lose my parents, my grandparents took a scared, grieving little boy and made my life as good as it could be under the circumstances. I hate like hell my parents were killed but am grateful every day that I had someone who was in my corner."

She pushed against him, and he loosened his grip, afraid of what he would see in her eyes. He'd always hated the pity that most people offered, especially when they had no idea what to say. She twisted around so that she could look directly at him. His heart pounded, and he felt sure she could hear it even with her ear no longer pressed against his chest. He needn't have worried. What greeted him were her beautiful eyes, filled with emotion but not pity.

"Oh, Ben, I had no idea, but now I understand how you relate to Charlie and Lily so well. I knew you were so close to Anna but had no idea she was your surrogate mother. And I knew she was special but had no idea how special."

"Don't you see, Violet? You're just as special."

"I'm just a mom—"

"No," he interrupted, not wanting her to downplay what she did. "There are other moms who would have ranted and raved about their husband's infidelity. Been so angry that it would have spewed out into everything in their lives, including their children. They would have cloaked themselves in self-pity, or loathing, or destructive behavior. But you… you've given your children the chance to remember the good parts of their father. You haven't tainted Lily's memories or Charlie's ideas of Matt. You've moved on, giving them a good life, being both mom and dad. They've learned how to deal with life and be resilient through you. That's a gift you cannot downplay or deny you've given."

She sucked in her lips and breathed heavily through her nose. Finally, swallowing deeply, she whispered, "You're a real boost for my ego."

His chest felt lighter and the tightness around his heart eased. Reaching up, he cupped her face, drawing her forward until their lips met. Slowly at first and then building, the flames threatening to consume. The need to devour her was strong but he tempered his desire, wanting to take care of her.

She pulled back, her breath ragged. "I haven't been with anyone since Matt. I'm not sure why that's important for me to tell you."

Her cheeks were blushed, and he wondered if it wasn't embarrassment as much as passion. "You can tell me anything that you want to. Anything that's important to you."

She shook her head slowly as though trying to gather her thoughts. "I guess I'm just nervous. I've only ever been with Matt, and looking back with all I know now…"

Understanding dawned, and he lifted her chin so that her eyes met his. "Violet, don't take on the doubts he gave you. I swear I am not a weak man. And my word is solid. There is no other woman in my life, and kissing you is better than anything I've ever felt before. I don't know where we're going or what you want to call us, but that's the whole point right now... whatever we are, we are an *us*. And as long as there is an *us*, then there will be no one else."

Her lips curved slowly, and her cheeks blushed even more. "So, you like kissing me?"

He moved closer, his mouth barely touching hers as he chuckled. Mumbling against her soft lips, he whispered, "Kissing you is like watching the dawn rise in a perfectly blue sky. Where you know the day is just beginning, anything is possible, and it will only get better."

Her hands snatched up to clutch his cheeks, and twisting her head, she latched onto his mouth. Now, there was no holding back. Soft and slow was a thing of the past. Teeth bumped. Tongues tangled. Breasts pressed against his chest. Her hot core ground against his swollen erection.

For a moment, he felt like a teenager fumbling in the backseat of his granddad's old station wagon. *Christ, she admitted her inexperience, and I'm treating her like I have no finesse.* But the reality was he'd never felt like this. Wanting everything all at once and yet wanting everything to be perfect for her. With the kids upstairs, they'd never be able to do what he wanted to do, which was strip her naked, kiss her entire body, and worship her as they came together. But with hands roaming and her kisses sending shockwaves throughout his body, centering on his heart, he was fine with just what they were doing right now.

His hands cupped her ass, pulling her tighter. Her short fingernails scraped along his scalp sending more tingles, his senses on overload. He glided one hand over her hip, dipping in at her waist, and around to cup her breasts, his thumb moving over her nipple. She groaned into his mouth, and he swallowed the sound, desperately wanting to hear her moan when he was buried deep inside of her. When his cock felt ready to explode, he slowly pushed her back, creating a separation between them that was only a few inches but felt like a mile.

"Christ, babe, I don't want to stop, but…"

"I know," she breathed heavily. "I'd love to take you upstairs…"

Now it was his turn to nod and say, "I know."

Her teeth landed on her bottom lip, swollen from his kisses, and he could tell she was deep in thought. "Don't overthink this, Violet."

She smiled again, and he knew if he could see that smile every day for the rest of his life he'd be happy. That and smiles from Lily and Charlie.

A shy expression crossed her face. "So, this starts *us*?"

"Absolutely."

"Ben, please, don't take this the wrong way, but I have to say it. It wouldn't be right if I don't."

"I told you, I want you to say anything that's important to you. You can tell me anything. You can ask me anything. If it's important to you, then it's important to me."

She nodded, her hands resting on his shoulders as

she sat straddling his lap. "I haven't been part of a couple in a long time. I haven't wanted to be. When I was with Matt, I thought it was the greatest thing ever. And when it was over and I discovered that so much of it was a lie, I wasn't sure I ever wanted to be part of a couple again. What I feel for you is real. But if it was just me taking this chance, that would be one thing. But it's Charlie and Lily, too."

"Believe me, I'm crazy about those two. I don't just see you and me as the *us* I'm referring to. I see it as you, me, Charlie, Lily, even Babciu... all of us together."

She dragged in another deep breath before letting it out slowly. "Does it seem too fast? I mean, my heart doesn't think so, but my mind is scared."

"I didn't expect this," he admitted. "I've never been around a lot of kids, but those two have wormed their way inside." He kissed her lips lightly before sliding his nibbles along her jaw until his mouth was at her ear. "We can go slow... see how the children feel about us. See how we feel about us."

She worried her bottom lip, so he gently placed his thumb over the abraded flesh, the warmth from their kisses still evident. "Tell me... what are you thinking?"

"One of the reasons I haven't dated was not wanting to subject my kids to men who might not be around for the right reasons or only want me but not them. You were different. You were a neighbor... then a friend. But I'm afraid they've set their sights on you, and I just don't want you to wake up and feel maneuvered."

"Shhh," he whispered, smiling. "I'm used to tactics... used to warfare... used to subterfuge. Believe me, it didn't take long for me to realize the kids were giving us time together. But that was fine by me. And I respect your choices as their mother to put them first in your life. I just want a chance to see if there's room for me as well."

She leaned forward and kissed along his jaw, the soft touch feather-light. His cock stirred, and he stood, lifting her with him.

"I'm going to go," he said, grinning at her mewl of discontent. "Cause if I don't, the kids might find me sleeping in your bed in the morning, and I know we're not ready for that."

They walked hand in hand to the back door where they stood for another long moment kissing once again. Finally, he stepped out, pleased when the security light came on and heard her click the lock behind him. Jogging through the yard, he scaled the fence and headed into his house, already planning the next day's activities. *A Sunday with everyone together.* It sounded perfect.

15

Ben had spent Sunday morning at Violet's house, painting the upstairs bathroom cabinets in thick, glossy white paint. Reminding the kids to use the downstairs powder room when they needed to use the bathroom, he shut the door to the one in Violet's bedroom to let the paint dry. She had spent the morning with his grandmother and Lily making cookies for the church before a friend came to drive Babciu to the meeting. Lily came back to play with Charlie while Violet left to make her weekly grocery shopping trip. When she suggested the kids go with her, they vetoed the idea, clambering to stay with Ben and help him work on the house.

He'd assured her that it was fine with him and it would give her a chance to make a trip out without having to corral the kids. Then, he took a chance and leaned in, kissing her quickly on the lips. Her eyes had widened before shooting her gaze toward the kids. He twisted his head to see Charlie and Lily standing next to each other watching them, smiles on both of their faces. Deciding not to make a big deal about the show of affection, he winked as Violet rolled her eyes, made the kids promise to be good, and left for the grocery store.

He could hear the children playing in the backyard with Bounder and headed down the stairs, deciding that he would see if they wanted a snack. Just as he made it to the kitchen, a piercing scream was heard and his heart jolted. Racing to the laundry room, he threw open the door and spied Lily lying on the grass, holding her foot with tears streaming down her face as she sobbed.

He tore out of the house, dropping to his knees beside her. "What happened?" One look at her ankle and he cursed under his breath. It was already swelling.

Charlie hopped around from one foot to the other, his face pinched with worry. "She was running. She was just running."

"Charlie, run and lock the kitchen door," he called out as he scooped Lily into his arms. She clung to him, still crying, and he felt a fear that had never shaken him when he was a SEAL. He'd seen men with gunshot and knife wounds, broken limbs, lacerations of all types, but his heart had never pounded as it did at that moment.

Charlie ran back to him, and he jogged out the gate of Violet's smaller yard, heading straight to his SUV. Throwing open the door, he placed her gently into the back seat before turning to heft Charlie in next to his sister. "I'll be right back. Gotta grab my wallet." He locked them inside before running through the back of his house and snagging his wallet from the counter. Opening the pantry, he pulled out a plastic zipper bag and filled it with ice. Locking the kitchen door, he raced back to his SUV and climbed in.

Twisting in his seat, he watched Lily's face, still scrunched in pain with tears running down her face, look at him with trust. "Sweetheart, I know it hurts, but try to hold this on your ankle. The ice will help, I promise."

"Ben, where are we going?" Charlie asked in a shaky voice.

One look and Ben knew Charlie was close to tears. "We're going to the emergency room. Lily's ankle might just be sprained, or it could be broken. But we need to have a doctor take a look at it." He started the engine and pulled out onto the street, forcing his breathing to steady and his heartbeat to slow while battling the urge to speed down the road.

"I want M-mom." Lily's voice hitched between tears, the sound stabbing straight through Ben.

"I'm going to call her right now," he promised. Connecting his phone through his vehicle, Violet didn't pick up so he left a message. "Babe, I don't want you to panic, but Lily's hurt her ankle. I'm taking her to St. Marguerite's Hospital Emergency Room. As soon as you get this message, meet us there."

Looking into the rearview mirror at Lily's tear-stained face, he said, "Hang on, Lily girl. It's going to be all right, I promise."

Ten minutes later, he parked and scooped Lily into his arms again, racing through the ER doors with Charlie at his side. It was in his nature to bark orders, his military training expecting them to be obeyed. Frustrated at the paperwork that needed to be completed, he sat in the waiting room with a sniffling Lily on his lap, her huge, swollen ankle propped up on the chair next to him with Charlie leaning against his legs, helping to fill in the information on the forms. Handing them to the woman at the admittance desk, he begged, "Please, get to her as soon as you can."

It only took another moment before a sweet-faced older nurse called them back. She glanced at Charlie with concern and looked at Ben. "Is there anyone else who came with you that can watch your son?"

"No, I'm the only one here."

She nodded and led them into the triage room where a young doctor that looked to be barely out of high school walked in, his smile wide. He joked with Lily as he examined her ankle, but she only glared, crying out when the prodding hurt.

"Do you have to do that?" Ben growled. "Can't you see the swelling?"

The doctor simply grinned as he winked at Lily. "I think your dad's getting a tad upset."

Ben leaned forward, checking the man's ID to make sure he was a real doctor. Seeing he was, he glared as Lily cried out again. "Do you have to keep hurting her?"

Lily sniffled and said, "You better not upset him. He was in the Navy." She turned her tear-stained face toward him. "Right?"

"That's right, baby," Ben said, forcing his voice to calm. Before he had a chance to question him again, the doctor got back to business.

"We'll need to take a picture of the inside of your

foot and ankle to see if there are any broken bones. I know you said you were playing outside, did you trip over anything?"

She shook her head, still wiping errant tears away from her eyes. "I think I stepped in a hole."

"A hole?" Ben asked, looking down at her.

She scrunched her nose and shrugged. "It just felt like the ground sank in when I was running."

Ben didn't ask any more questions but sat in the hard plastic chair holding her hand with Charlie in his lap. The technicians came to roll her down the hall to the x-ray room, and he promised he'd be right there when she got back.

"Don't worry, honey," one of the technicians said. "We're just going to take some pictures and then we'll bring you right back here to Daddy."

She had only been gone for a moment when Violet rounded the corner and bolted into the room. Before he had a chance to speak, her eyes darted around before landing on him. "Lily? Where is she?"

He stood with Charlie balanced on his hip, the little boy's arms clinging to his neck. Taking the two steps it took to get to her, he reached out with his free hand and pulled her close. "It's okay. They've just taken her to x-ray."

"They told her all about it, Mom. They said it's just like having a picture taken, and it won't hurt."

She reached out her arms, and Charlie let go of Ben, allowing his mom to pull him close. She closed her eyes and held him tight, taking a deep breath and letting it out slowly. Ben wrapped both of his arms around the two of them, hating the reason they were there but loving the fact that he could offer comfort.

"What happened?" she asked, her gaze looking over Charlie's shoulder to him.

"I'm not sure. They were in the backyard playing with the dog when I suddenly heard her scream. I had just made it downstairs and raced out and she was lying on the ground with her ankle already swelling. I had no idea if it was just sprained or broken, but I wanted to get her here."

She leaned in close, dropping her forehead to his chest while still keeping Charlie clutched in her arms. He kissed the top of her head and she finally focused on Charlie. "Did you see what happened?"

"I think she stepped in a hole."

She blinked and gave a little shake of her head. "A hole? I don't think we have holes in our yard, Charlie."

Charlie said, "Probably because of the bad man that's in the yard."

Ben's gaze shot toward Violet, finding her staring at him, her expression just as confused as his. Before they had a chance to ask Charlie more questions, the sound of Lily's bed being rolled back into the room met their ears.

"Sweetie!"

"Mom!"

Violet easily transferred Charlie back to Ben's arms as she leaned down and hugged Lily. He lowered Charlie to the ground and bent to kiss Lily's head, glad to see she was no longer crying.

The nurse came in and explained that the doctor had

ordered pain medication for Lily and he'd be in soon to discuss the x-ray findings. Violet sat on the edge of the bed with her daughter and Ben sat in the hard chair, Charlie balancing on his knees.

Ben's eyes had closed for just a moment, but they opened at Charlie's soft question. "Did you hear what that nurse called me?"

"What she called you?" Ben looked at the shy smile aimed his way.

"She called me your son."

Ben's gaze darted up to see Violet staring back at the two of them. A giggle from a pain-free Lily slipped out, and they both swung their heads toward her as well.

"One of the ladies who rolled me back to x-ray said that my dad was handsome. The other one said he was a hunk." She giggled again. "What's a hunk?"

Looking back at Violet, he shook his head, rushing to assure, "I didn't identify myself as their dad, but they made the assumption—"

"Oh, my goodness, it's fine." Violet waved her hand in the air in a dismissive gesture. "I'm sure that must've felt weird for you, but the most important thing was just getting help for Lily."

"I wish you were my daddy," Lily said, a yawn stretching her face.

"Me too," Charlie piped up. "It made me feel good when they called me your son."

Violet's shocked expression met his and her mouth opened for what Ben was sure was going to be a rebuttal. With a shake of his head, he silenced her and hoped she understood that Lily and Charlie's words had not upset him. Quite the contrary, warmth spread throughout him as a feeling of gratitude and peace speared his heart.

The teenage-looking doctor walked in again, his smile still wide. "Okay, how's the little lady?" He patted her good leg after greatly exaggerating his decision as to which leg was injured. Lily giggled, Violet smiled, the doctor beamed, and Ben battled a grimace.

"Looks like the pain medicine has kicked in." He walked to the computer and tapped away for a moment before turning to Violet and Ben. "The good news is that her ankle isn't broken, but the bad news is that she has a moderate sprain. And often, a sprain causes more pain than a fracture. She didn't tear any ligaments, and in young children, their bodies are still developing. Her recovery will be much shorter than an adult."

"What should we do?" Violet asked, her hand resting on Lily.

"The nurse will be in with your discharge instructions, but essentially, elevate, ice packs, and compression. We'll send her home in a compression boot. For pain, just over-the-counter pain medicine will work." He looked down at Lily and smiled again, rubbing his hands together as though getting ready to impart the knowledge of the world. "And no running until it's healed. No dancing, twirling, hopping, skipping, jump-roping, sky-diving, or cave exploring! For several days, she shouldn't put pressure on it at all, then she can allow it to bear weight as she is comfortable while still being very careful." He tweaked Lily's nose then headed out of the ER bay, whistling.

"He's goofy," Lily said, yawning widely again.

Ben agreed but kept his opinion to himself. Thirty minutes later the nurse had come in and reviewed the discharge instructions and fitted Lily with a compression boot. "Oh, you'll need to stop at the reception desk on your way out since your husband didn't have his insurance card with him," she said to Violet as she left.

Ben stood, setting Charlie's feet onto the floor. Violet stifled a grin and shook her head. Walking over, she placed her hand on Ben's arm and said, "I can't begin to thank you enough for being there."

"You don't have to thank me, Violet. I want to be here for them and am just glad that I was." Looking past her to where Lily was sitting up in bed, he said, "Let's get everybody home."

While the hospital staff rolled Lily out in a wheelchair, Ben and Charlie went to the parking lot to get Violet's car. Lifting Lily out of the chair, he gently placed her in the back of the car and made sure she was buckled with her legs stretched out on the seat to stay elevated. Turning back to Violet, he said, "I'll follow behind with Charlie and get her settled inside. Don't worry about the groceries, I'll get those in as well. If anything thawed or melted, I'll dump them in the trash, and then Charlie and I can go back out."

"What about Anna? I forgot she was at a meeting."

"Don't worry about it. She was already getting a ride home with her friend, and I've already called her to tell her what was going on. She's in the kitchen making sandwiches for everyone, and once we get settled in your house, I'll have her come over."

"I know you said I don't have to thank you, but... I'm so used to doing everything by myself—"

"Well, now, you've got me." Lifting his hand, he smoothed his knuckles over Violet's cheek, feeling the tense muscles underneath his fingers. "It'll be fine. I promise."

It didn't take long for the group to settle into Violet's house with Lily on the sofa, her foot propped up with a pillow. Charlie ran to gather toys and books for his sister to play with, and Ben escorted Babciu over, bringing sandwiches, chips, and cookies.

After eating, he excused himself and went out into the backyard, stalking to the place where Lily had fallen. He knelt, moving around on his knees with his hands pressed to the grass. Bounder thought it was a game and trotted all around, his nose buried as he sniffed the area. The ground gave way underneath his hand, and he could see the impression in the soft earth where she twisted her ankle. Sitting back on his heels, he stared, confusion filling him. *What the hell? Moles?* He'd never seen mole trails in their yards, but then he hadn't been back in Hope City for very long. And as a child, he wouldn't have noticed them.

Continuing to crawl around as he followed Bounder's sniffing trail, he found a few more places where the ground gave way underneath his hand. He'd warn Charlie to be careful until he had a chance to figure out what caused the holes. *It's the bad man.* Charlie's words came back but he still had no idea what the little boy's nightmares had to do with the backyard. Pushing to a stand, he stalked inside, smiling at the sight that greeted him in Violet's living room. She and Lily were on the sofa, his grandmother sat in the comfy chair nearby, Charlie was giving a great description of the hospital's emergency room as he acted out the part of the doctor, and Bounder trotted over to lay on the floor.

Violet looked up as he entered and smiled. She scooted closer to Lily, giving him room to slide in next to her on the sofa. With his arm around her, smiles from Babciu settling like a warm blanket, and Lily and Charlie safe, he breathed easier than he had in a long time.

16

That evening, after Ben had walked Babciu back to their house, he returned to carry Lily up the stairs to her bedroom. Violet smiled as they walked in. "I'll get her changed and then you can come back in and say good-night," she suggested.

"I'll corral Charlie while you do that."

"Oh, you don't have to—"

"Not a question of having to, babe." He winked, and as he turned to walk out, she stopped him with her hand on his arm.

Lifting on her toes, she whispered, "You're like a knight that's just ridden up on a white horse." Glancing over her shoulder at Lily, she added, "I can tell she thinks the same thing." Holding his gaze, she continued. "I know it doesn't have to be forever, but thank you for that, Ben. It's been a long time since she's believed in a white knight."

He kissed her lightly, winked at Lily, and walked into Charlie's bedroom, grinning at the retro-Batman pajamas. The little boy's energy was fading, and he crawled into bed with no complaints, yawning widely.

"You gonna be able to sleep?" Ben pulled the covers over Charlie's small frame.

Rolling to his side, Charlie nodded. "Yeah, I'm tired." He scrunched his face and asked, "Did you find anything in the yard?"

"Yeah, I found some small holes. It might be moles... they like to dig under the ground. Maybe they come from the park across the street."

Charlie glanced toward his window overlooking the backyard before peering up at Ben again. "Will the light come on if someone's out there?"

"Yeah, buddy, but if the moles are under the ground, the light won't detect them so it won't come on."

Charlie's nose scrunched as his expression turned pensive.

Ben's brow lowered, and he rubbed his chin while sitting on the side of Charlie's bed trying to figure out what to say. He didn't want to discount nightmares, but also didn't want Charlie worrying over something that wasn't real. "Well, buddy, remember how we talked about the sensor able to detect motion?" Gaining Charlie's nod, he continued, "Even though a dream can feel real, it's not. Therefore, the motion detector won't go on when you're having a nightmare."

"But it's not a nightmare." Charlie sat up in bed, his brow crinkled. "I saw him."

"You saw him in your imagination?"

"No, in the backyard looking for something."

A trickle of unease slithered through Ben as his gaze

moved from the serious child to the window over-looking the backyards and then back to Charlie. "How did you see him from here?"

"I got out of bed and looked out the window. Then I got scared and ran back to bed."

Ben heard a noise at the door and swung his gaze around to see Violet standing there, her eyes wide. She was doing the same thing he had been—her gaze moved from Charlie to the window and back again.

"Baby," Violet began, walking into the room and sitting on the opposite side of the bed, "when I would come in, you'd just tell me about being scared of the bad man. You never said you looked out your window at him."

Charlie shrugged, his fingers fiddling with the covers. "I figured you might get mad if I was out of bed."

Violet leaned forward and wrapped her arms around him, kissing the top of his head. "I always want you to tell me what is going on. That's the only way I can make sure I'm taking care of you."

After a moment, Charlie began to squirm and Violet let go, allowing him to snuggle back under the covers. Bending, she kissed his cheek before pulling the covers up to his ears. Ben leaned over and ruffled his hair, then reached his hand out toward Violet and they walked hand-in-hand out of Charlie's room. With the night-light in the corner and the hall light left on, there was plenty of illumination for Charlie to see that he had nothing to be afraid of.

Neither spoke as they made their way downstairs, but as soon as his feet landed on the first floor, he led

Violet into the kitchen before dropping her hand and stalking to the door leading to the backyard. Flipping on the light, he moved out onto the steps and the security light came on, illuminating the whole backyard. Hands on his hips, he stared at the small expanse of grass and fence, moving his gaze from the sidewalk next to the street to the place where Lily had fallen.

The sliver of unease that had moved through him earlier grew. He tried to imagine what Charlie had seen —if someone had actually been in the yard, and if so, what the hell they were doing that made indentions in the ground?

A gentle touch of hands on his waist had him suck in his breath as Violet moved behind him, gliding her arms around as she pressed her front to his back. Her soft floral scent surrounded him, offering a small bit of comfort with his turbulent thoughts. They stood silent for a moment with his hands holding hers at his abs, and then he reached around to guide her to his side.

"What are you thinking?" she asked, her voice barely above a whisper.

"I was going to ask you the same thing."

Both fell silent and the only sounds heard were the traffic on the parallel roads fronting Anna and Violet's townhouses with a rare vehicle traveling on the smaller road next to them.

"I was so sure Charlie was dreaming." Sighing heavily, she lifted her face to his. "I comforted him but never thought that he might have seen someone out here. I know this sounds terrible, but I'm still not quite sure. God, now I feel so guilty."

He looked down and squeezed her waist. "Don't take that on. You're a wonderful mother and it's not hard to imagine he was having a nightmare."

"Why would someone come here? To break into the house? God, that's so scary. But there's nothing of value here. Maybe it was a vagrant searching through the garbage?"

"I don't know," he said, his mind turning over possibilities but coming up empty. "But, tomorrow, I'm going over this yard carefully. If there has been someone out here, I want to know why... and who."

———

The next day was sunny but the weather didn't match anyone's disposition. Lily was in pain and grumpy, and Ben finally carried her over to give his grandmother a chance to pamper her. It also served to give Violet a chance to run back to the grocery store to replace the frozen items that had thawed in her car while she was at the emergency room. Ben offered, but Violet wanted to pick up Lily's favorites.

Charlie had wanted to play with a friend, but the other mom had to cancel at the last minute, and he was sitting in the living room, his arms crossed over his chest as he pouted.

"Come on, Charlie. Let's take a look at the backyard to see if we can discover what made the holes."

The little boy's head popped up and his eyes widened as much as the smile that spread over his face. "Like we can play detectives looking for clues?"

"Absolutely."

Now, he and Charlie were moving over the back-yard with a purpose. "So, what did you see the man do when you looked out your window?"

"He was bent over." Charlie mimicked a man stooping as he moved along.

"Okay…" Ben nodded, although he still had no idea why someone would be stooping in the yard. "Did he have anything in his hands?"

Charlie scrunched his nose in thought then shrugged his thin shoulders. "Don't know. It was dark."

"Was it a man or maybe a teenager?"

Charlie looked up and shaded his eyes from the sun with his hand as he stared into Ben's face. "I think it was a man… but I don't know. Why would a teenager want to be in our yard?"

Patting Charlie on the shoulder, Ben sighed. "I don't know, buddy. I don't know why anyone would want to be in the yard."

Ben continued to carefully make his way around the small yard, discovering four other places where the ground appeared to have been disturbed. Closer investigation allowed him to see where areas of sod had been lifted and the dirt disturbed underneath and the sod replaced. Sitting back on his heels while Charlie climbed over the fence into Babciu's yard to play with Bounder, Ben scrubbed his hand over the back of his neck. *Someone was here.*

Standing, he stared at the yard like a SEAL staring at the ground searching for IEDs. There was no pattern to the holes, although they were spread out over a ten-foot square area that was not close to the house.

The ground didn't appear to have been shoveled, more like a piece of sod had been lifted and a pole inserted, rocked back and forth, loosening the earth about a foot deep before the sod had been replaced. *Nothing was buried here, so he must have been searching. No way was this a teen... had to have been an adult who was specifically and systematically looking for something.*

Babciu came to the back door and waved toward him. Jumping over the fence, he jogged up to where she stood. "Everything okay?"

"Yes, of course. Lily's resting comfortably and is watching TV. I see Violet is back from the store?"

He looked over his shoulder to see Violet carrying a few groceries through her backdoor after waving toward them. His grandmother's hand on his arm drew his attention back to her.

"I'd like you and Violet to go out to have a nice lunch... or stay in for lunch... whatever. I'm fixing my special grilled cheese sandwiches for Charlie and Lily and would love for you and Violet to have a little time to yourselves."

His breath caught in his throat at the offer. He knew exactly how he wanted to spend the little time... with his arms around Violet and his lips on hers. Reining himself in, he blew out a long breath. "I don't know how she'll feel about—"

"I've already discovered the kids are excited about my special grilled cheese sandwiches, and I called Violet while she was still at the grocery and she's more than happy to have some time with the kids here."

Blinking, he stared at the little smile curving his grandmother's lips. "I... you..." He shook his head. "Aren't you kind of sneaky?"

She laughed and patted his shoulder. "Go on... have a nice time. The kids are safe right here."

Looking over his shoulder again, he saw Violet through the kitchen window, smiling at him. Bending to kiss his grandmother's cheek, he trotted down the deck stairs and across the yard, vaulting over the fence, and then picking up speed as he raced through Violet's backdoor. His feet stuttered to a halt when she came into view. Standing in the kitchen, she looked much like she had when she left for the store... and different. Same jeans that hugged her hips and legs, and yet now it was hard to take his eyes away from her curves. Same pink T-shirt that now seemed to cast a rosy glow over her cheeks. Same ponytail, and yet now his fingers itched to pull out the band and let the waves cascade down.

Her fingers were clasped in front of her as though she had no idea what to do with her hands. He stalked closer, and her head dropped back as her eyes remained on his. Stopping when their toes were almost touching, he lifted his hand and cupped her face. "I guess you heard Babciu has the kids for a while."

She nodded, her eyes bright and her smile curving her lips.

"There are no expectations here, Violet. We can sit

and eat a sandwich. We can lounge on the sofa and talk, or—"

"I don't want to talk."

His thumb had smoothed over her cheek but now held perfectly still. He said nothing, giving full control over to her.

Her tongue darted out and licked her bottom lip. "I don't want to eat. I don't want to talk. I want to kiss."

He grinned and drew her closer. Her hands moved to his arms, gliding up his biceps to his shoulders, her fingers digging in slightly. His lips had barely skimmed hers in a soft kiss when she mumbled against his lips.

"I want more than a kiss, Ben. I want whatever you want to give."

He moved back an inch and held her gaze. "You have to be careful what you wish for, babe. I know what I want with you, but you're in control here. You need to let me know what you want."

Without hesitation, she lifted on her toes and wrapped her hands around the back of his neck, pulling him down so that their lips met once again. He wanted nothing more than to plunge into her warm mouth, kissing her until he was the only thing she could see and feel.

Mumbling against his lips again, she said, "I want to keep kissing you, but I want you to take me upstairs. We might only have an hour, but I want it to be an hour together in my bed."

His heart threatened to beat out of his chest, and he bent, sliding one arm below her ass and scooping her up. Moving quickly, he mounted the steps and turned at the top of the stairs to head into her bedroom. Just to make sure they wouldn't be surprised, he closed the door and clicked the lock.

Carrying Violet to the bed, he slowly let her legs fall free until her feet touched the floor. Still uncertain, he hesitated and stared down into her beautiful face, hoping she wouldn't but wanting her to feel free to stop anything she wasn't comfortable with.

The only thing that greeted him was her wide smile just before she pulled him down for another kiss.

17

As Violet gave herself over to the kiss, she was sure. Sure of Ben. Sure of them. Allowing herself a few seconds to cast her mind into the past, she couldn't remember being this sure even with Matt. They'd been so young when they began. He was her first kiss. Her first everything. In fact, she'd only kissed one other man. A year ago, allowing herself to be set up on a blind date, she'd been miserable during the entire dinner, and shocked when the man pulled her in for a good night kiss. Now, Ben's lips erased all other thoughts.

He lowered her slowly until just her toes touched the floor, her front gliding along his. His hands moved up her sides, skimming her breasts until he moved further and held her cheeks. Letting him guide the kiss, she felt a slight pressure that angled her head, giving him deeper access. As though every cell in her body was electrified, her senses were heightened. Thick muscles met her fingertips as she clung to his arms. The height difference only served to make her feel more surrounded as he bent toward her. He slid a jean-clad thigh between her parted legs, and her hot core felt the friction.

His lips were soft and forceful. His hands were gentle and claiming. Her soft curves were pressed against the hard planes of his body. And she was very aware of his erection pressing against her tummy, unable to stop from grinding against his thigh.

She slid her hands down to the bottom of his T-shirt, aware of the muscles and desperately wanting to feel skin. Slipping her fingers underneath the soft cotton, she trailed along the dips and curves, dragging his shirt upward along with her hands. When the material would go no further, he separated from her lips just long enough to reach behind and grabbed the T-shirt, jerking it over his head and down his arms, tossing it to the side. Before she had a chance to admire the tanned skin covering hardened muscles, he was clutching her again, the kiss taking away all other thoughts.

She was barely aware when his hands moved over her body the same way that hers had caressed his. His fingers slipped underneath her T-shirt, and she felt each touch like a fiery brand. The material glided up and over her breasts, and they once again separated so he could pull the garment over her head and raised arms before it landed in a crumpled pile on the floor as well.

His eyes skimmed over her torso, snagging on her breasts before he lowered his lips and kissed along the mounds covered by satin and lace. She spent little on herself but had found a discount store with pretty albeit inexpensive lingerie. Now, his eyes flaring just before his lips dropped to her breasts, she was glad that she was wearing the soft pink bra. He bent deeper, and with his arms around her waist, lifted her into the air, her feet dangling as his lips closed over her satin-covered nipple. If she thought her body was electrified before, it was nothing compared to the tingling she now felt.

So lost in the sensations, she was surprised when he lowered her and discovered they were at her bed. Bent deeply at the waist, he trailed kisses from her breasts over her tummy as his fingers unbuttoned her jeans. The expression on his face seemed reverent, and her breath caught in her throat at his slow gentleness. He wasn't rushing. He wasn't trying to jerk her clothes off just to get her naked. He slowly undid her zipper, and his fingers trailed over her warm skin before dipping into the waistband of her jeans and panties.

She lifted her hips as he dragged them over her ass and down her legs before they disappeared onto the floor. Now, naked, she was suddenly overcome with how her body had changed since becoming a mom. It was one thing for Matt to have seen her considering her husband had witnessed all the body changes that came with pregnancy. But even he had not been faithful.

"Hey, come back to me."

At those words, her gaze jumped up to Ben's face, concern filling his eyes.

"Where did you go, babe?"

"I'm sorry. I'm a little self-conscious." Her fingers fluttered nervously over her belly. "I can't pretend or hide that I have a mom body. I'm not ashamed of it, but it's just... well... you should know that you're the first man to see me naked since my husband. There's been no one else I've been with except him."

Without saying a word, he toed off his shoes and unbuckled his jeans, shucking them and his boxers in one swift movement. He crawled over her body and shifted to the side. With his elbow crooked and his head resting in his hand, he lay one heavy thigh over hers, and with his free hand glided his fingers through her hair, touching her soft cheek, never taking his eyes from hers. "You have no idea how glad I am that you don't play games. Everything about you is honest. And that's what you deserve."

His warm breath moved over her face and she craved his words as much as she craved his body.

"I can't fathom how a man who's made a vow of forever with a woman, any woman, but especially one like you, who carried and gave birth to his children, would walk away or even be tempted by something else. But you've got to remember what I said about him being the weak link. That's not on you, Violet. A man like that doesn't stray because your body changed. A man like that strays because *he* is weak."

As he spoke, his hand drifted over her shoulder, gliding over her breast with his thumb gently circling her nipple before continuing its downward path until his hand rested over her belly. "You… every inch of you is beautiful. I see it. I know it. And I promise you, I am not weak. You can trust in that, and you can trust in me."

Tears filled her eyes and she battled to keep them from falling, but one slipped from each eye, trailing down to the comforter underneath. He leaned forward and kissed each tear-path before sealing his lips over her mouth again. At that moment, she vowed to let go of the past. Her marriage and Matt's infidelity held no power over her anymore. All she wanted was Ben.

She twisted slightly so she was facing him, placing her hot core against his thigh. He groaned and his hand began to roam over her body, his movements more urgent while remaining gentle. His hand moved over her mound, pressing against her clit, and her body jerked, sensitive and primed. It only took a moment once his finger slid through her folds and entered her channel, tweaking deep inside before her whole body tightened. Like a coiled snake ready to strike, she cried out against his mouth as her body jerked in response. Her orgasm, the first non-self-induced one in years, had taken her not only to the edge but had flung her over into the abyss. But instead of being a scary place of doubts and insecurities, it was a safe place to land in his arms.

His fingers skimmed upward, his palm cupping her breast at the same time he sucked the other nipple deeply into his mouth. Kisses, licks, nips, and sucks were driving her wild and she clung to him, wanting more, wanting everything.

His body felt heavy as he shifted over her, but she welcomed his weight. Lifting up on his forearms, he dipped his head to take her lips in a searing kiss as her fingers dug into his back, urging him on. Finally, when she was ready to beg, he pushed up further and reached into his wallet that he'd tossed onto the bed when he shucked his jeans. Pulling out a condom, she listened to the sound of the tearing foil, eagerly watching as he rolled it over his impressive cock.

He palmed his erection and held her gaze, and just as she nearly wept with desire and need, he leaned back down, placing the tip at her entrance. "You're still in control, babe."

"Good," she groaned. "I want you now."

His smile spread across his face, spearing her heart. Spreading her thighs, she dragged her heels up over his muscular ass just as he drove deep into her sex.

"Christ, you feel so good. So fuckin' tight and so good," he moaned as he slid out before thrusting in again.

After having two children, she couldn't imagine how she felt tight to him, but as his cock filled her, she had to admit it was delicious. Keeping his weight off her chest, his forearms were planted on either side of her shoulders, his fingers tangling in her hair. She closed her eyes and let the age-old dance of thrust and parry fill her senses. Her fingers gripped his shoulders, then her short fingernails dragged along his scalp before returning to his arms. Her hips caught his rhythm and met him with each thrust.

His masculine scent blended with her floral shampoo, and mixed with the heady odor of their desire created a blend that was uniquely their own. With every movement, her inner muscles coiled tighter, and her fingernails dug in a little deeper.

"Open your eyes," he commanded, his voice more guttural than gentle.

She acquiesced and found him staring straight at her, his mesmerizing gaze holding her focus. Her top teeth landed on her bottom lip as the muscles inside tightened even more before suddenly springing loose, shockwaves scattering throughout all of her nerves. Almost as though he'd been waiting for her, he thrust deeply several more times, and she watched as his neck muscles tightened, the veins standing in stark relief, and through clenched teeth, he groaned through his own release. He continued to pump more slowly until finally falling on top of her.

His weight was heavy, pressing her into the soft mattress, but she didn't mind. The weight made everything feel more real. After a moment of his ragged breathing, he shifted slightly to the side, pulling her with him so they lay face-to-face. Neither spoke for several minutes, their heartbeats pounding as they sucked in deep breaths.

His arms tightened, and he pulled her in close, her cheek resting on his chest as he kissed the top of her head. His thigh lay between hers, and his arms wrapped around her protectively. After listening to his heartbeat for several long moments, she finally leaned back and kissed the underside of his jaw before moving to his lips. This time the kiss was long and languid. More emotional and less frantic. The kiss of sated lovers.

"I owe my babcia," he said softly.

"I'm not sure how I'm going to face her, knowing that she knows… or thinks she might know… or if she doesn't know—"

He chuckled as he kissed her ramblings away. "Don't

worry," he assured. "She wouldn't have offered if she didn't like the idea of us together."

"Are we?" Her words were so soft, she wondered if she just thought them or had said them. At his jerk and narrowed-eyed gaze, she felt sure she had said them aloud. "It's just that sex doesn't always mean the same things for both partners."

His face softened, and he kissed her forehead then rested his lips there. The warmth of his mouth against her skin eased the pounding nerves that skittered through her stomach.

"Violet, I might not have been a man of many words, but I can see that it's hard for you to trust—"

"No, Ben, I trust you!" The idea slammed into her that he might get tired of always reassuring her that he was not like Matt.

"Babe, shhh." He kissed her lightly again. "What I was going to say is that I will do everything I can to not just tell you that you can trust me but I'll do everything I can to show you that you can trust me. Okay?"

She nodded, her gaze held by his.

"And when I said we were an *us*, that's not just you and me and sex. That's all of us. Sex is part of it, but only part of what we are together. And I know this is a lot, so we'll take it slow. Let the kids get used to us being together without being in their faces."

"I should warn you," she said, "but the kids are going to love us being together. I just don't want it to be too much for you."

His lips curved and his gaze never wavered. "Babe, it'll never be too much for me."

18

Two weeks later, Ben looked around the table, his heart lighter than it had been in a long time. Ensconced in a private room of a family restaurant, their group could celebrate Violet's graduation with ease and not be afraid of encroaching on the dinner enjoyment of other patrons. Babciu sat next to him with Violet's mom on the other side of her and Violet's dad at the end. Charlie and Lily sat close to their grandparents, soaking up the attention. With Violet next to him, their group was complete.

Lily was no longer in the compression boot, but he'd wrapped her ankle in an elastic bandage, securing it with clips. She insisted she didn't need to be carried, but he'd kept an eye on her. It wasn't needed though, considering her grandfather doted on her, assisting her as they made their way into the restaurant. Charlie was full of tales to his grandparents, but Ben noticed he said nothing about the *bad man in the yard*.

Violet's parents lived in one of the older neighborhoods in the north part of Hope City, where houses were set back from the road and tall trees graced the yards. At least that was how Violet described her child-hood home. He'd get to see it tomorrow since Roger and Daisy were taking the kids for an overnight stay, and he and Violet would pick them up in the afternoon.

That thought alone made him slide his hand over to cover Violet's, resting on the table. The idea that they could have an entire night and morning all to them-selves. Giving her hand a little squeeze, she immediately glanced toward him, a smile playing about her lips and her eyes gleaming. It might have been the lights from the restaurant but he liked to think it was because she was as excited about their night together as he was.

Roger stood and their attention moved to the other end of the table. Her father was not overly tall but held himself with a confident air as his warm gaze moved around the others gathered, finally landing on Violet as he lifted his glass of iced tea. "We're here to celebrate the graduation of my daughter. You've worked hard over the past years, and your mom and I are so proud of you—"

"And me?" Charlie asked, holding his glass of milk the way his grandfather was.

Everyone laughed and Roger's smile landed on Charlie as he nodded. "Yes, we are proud of you and Lily as well. You all have worked hard and accomplished so much. So, here's to Charlie, who is soon to finish first grade, Lily, who will finish fourth, and Violet, who now has her bachelor's degree."

Ben's fingers trailed a slow path over her shoulder as

his gaze stayed riveted on her. A blush graced her cheeks, and her pink-slicked lips curved into a smile. Ever since she had received her last grade the week before and her advisor confirmed her transcript for graduation, he'd felt her spirit lighten and knew part of her burden was lifted.

Everyone participated in the toast, but Roger stayed standing. Now, he looked toward Ben. "And let me just say that it's been a pleasure to get to know you and Anna. We are so glad you are part of their lives."

Another drink accompanied this toast and soon the server came with the check. Ben had planned to cover the check, but Roger had cornered him earlier at Violet's house before they left for dinner.

"Ben, I know you're the kind of man who plans on picking up the tab tonight, but I'm going to ask that you let me get it. You can take Violet out for drinks afterward if you want, but... well, her mom and I really want to do this for them. For all of you. Violet tells us how much you have helped her and the kids—"

"Sir, you don't owe me anything for being with them."

Roger had nodded, but grimaced. "I know, but it's just that we're so glad to see her happy again. When Matt died... and then..."

He'd placed his hand on Roger's shoulder, hoping to offer comfort to the struggling man. "Sir, I can only imagine your grief and pain for your daughter and grandchildren. And then your anger."

Roger had sucked in a deep breath through his nose before letting it out slowly. "That's it, Ben. You've hit the nail on the head. It was unbelievable grief and then followed by such anger. And I didn't want to show that anger to Violet. Her mother and I wanted to be supportive, but we struggled so with our anger toward him... and it's hard to express fury at a deceased man." Shaking his head slightly, he'd added, "I'm sorry. I never meant to go down this road with you. Daisy and I've heard all about you for weeks from Charlie and Lily. They are taken with you."

"And I'm crazy about them, too. It's still early days in our relationship, but I give you my word as a SEAL that I will always have their best intentions at heart."

Roger finally smiled and the two men shook hands. So now, as much as Ben didn't want to accept Roger's offer, he stepped back and allowed Violet's parents to treat them to dinner. Once they made it to the vehicles, Violet was busy with the kids, making sure they had their overnight bags for their sleepover with their grandparents. Lily stood next to her grandmother, who was talking to his babcia, holding her hand while Charlie bounced around.

Finally, the kids hugged their mom with promises to behave and they'd see her tomorrow. Surprisingly, they both hurried to Babciu, hugging her as well, careful of her cane and making sure to not cause her to lose balance. Ben's heart swelled as he watched them before glancing to see Violet's tremulous smile as well.

Charlie and Lily let go of Babciu and rushed over to him, throwing their arms around him, this time giving in to their exuberance. His arms encircled them as he squatted to their level. Stinging pricked his eyes, and he couldn't remember the last time he'd felt tearful. "You two be good for your grandparents," he said. As they leaned back to offer their assurances, he winked. "And have fun!"

Bouncing over to the car, they climbed into the back seat and waved as Roger and Daisy pulled out into the street.

"My word, your children are beautiful," his grandmother said, taking Violet's arm as they walked toward Ben's SUV.

Violet laughed. "Oh, Anna, I was going to say they are overwhelming!"

"It often feels overwhelming, but you're a wonderful mother and your children are delightful."

Ben assisted his grandmother into the back seat before escorting Violet to the passenger side.

"I hate that you have to take me home before you two go out for drinks," his babcia said.

He smiled into the rearview mirror. "I wouldn't have it any other way."

Soon, he walked into the house with her and made sure she was settled for the night. Ensuring she had her phone near the bed, she shooed them away with calls to have a good time and she'd see them in the morning.

Violet blushed as Ben hustled her back out to the SUV. "I feel so naughty!"

He nuzzled her ear, whispering, "I like you naughty." Closing her door, he hurried around the front and climbed behind the steering wheel. Twisting his body, he stared at her face, illuminated with only the streetlight on the corner. She was beautiful, and with her gaze locked on him as well, he slid his hand to the back of her neck and drew her forward as he leaned over. Her lips tasted of wine and dessert and he drank her in. As the kiss ended, she was slow to open her eyes, her face peaceful as she smiled.

"What are you thinking, babe?"

She ran her tongue over her bottom lip and sighed. "So much, Ben, I could burst with everything on my mind."

"Break it down for me."

She sucked in a deep breath, then let it out slowly. "Okay. I was thinking about how much more time I'll have with the kids, and you, and even my parents now that I am finished with classes."

"That's a good thing, but you forgot someone. You. You will now have more time for just you."

At that reminder, her smile widened, and she leaned forward to kiss him again. "Thank you for that, Ben. You're right."

"Okay, what else?"

"Umm, well, I was thinking that I can now officially look for a better job. And I know this sounds crazy, but I'm not looking for the greatest job in the world. Maybe that makes me sound like I don't care, but I want something that pays the bills and allows me to save some money. A job that is interesting but not overly stressful. A job that doesn't mind me being a mom and is understanding if there is a sick child or a school event that I need to get to." She hesitated, her brow crinkling. "Does that sound terrible? Like I don't care?"

"Violet, you know what that tells me? It tells me that

the most important thing in your life is Charlie and Lily. And you want a good job that utilizes your skills but is never going to be the most important thing to you. So, you look until you find something that fits what you need." He watched as she heaved another sigh and realized it was in relief. "Okay, what else?"

"I'm glad you got to meet my parents tonight."

He cocked his head to the side, waiting to see what else she was going to say. As usual, she didn't keep him guessing.

"They're important to me... important to Lily and Charlie. But so are you. And, well, I guess that I wanted them to meet the man who has become... um... important." She giggled. "That was a lot of *importants* all at once, wasn't it?"

He loved to hear her laugh. A little giggle or a belly laugh, it didn't matter. Her smile lit the room and filled his heart. "I'm glad you wanted me to meet them. I'm glad you feel strongly enough about what we're building that you wanted us to get to know each other. And I'm glad I'm important to you, 'cause the feelings I have for you are real and growing, and I don't see them going anywhere."

"Okay," she whispered, her lips still curving.

"Okay," he agreed. Turning, he started the engine and pulled onto the street. "Do you have any place special picked out for us to grab a drink?"

She shook her head. "With two kids, I never go out for drinks. I'll gladly let you make the choice."

"There's a pub off the Inner Harbor that's a decent place to go. It's out of the way so that it's not overrun by tourists. I've only been a couple of times when in town on leave. But I remember it's near one of the precincts, so there's usually a lot of first responders there."

"That sounds good, let's try it. What's the name of the pub?"

"The Celtic Cock."

Violet stared for a second, then burst into laughter. "Really?"

"It's my understanding that it's owned by a brother and sister who got it from their grandfather when he retired. Their grandfather's family had owned the pub in Ireland. I've been to a few pubs when I was in the British Isles that had great names." They parked along one of the streets near the harbor and walked along the area with trendy shops on one side and the water lapping against the concrete pylons on the other. Street-lamps were on, offering plenty of light for those out wandering along the waterfront. Turning down a side street, they walked for several more blocks until he looked up and pointed. "There it is."

Hanging over the door was a heavy wooden sign of a rooster enclosed in a Celtic circle. The words Celtic Cock were carved underneath.

"Oh, my gosh, you're right. That name and the sign are fabulous."

He pushed open the door and held it for her, his fingers resting along her lower back as he guided her through the bar. It was just as he remembered it. A large space with plenty of room for friends to gather. High top tables were along one side near the exposed brick wall. Heavy paneling was on the back wall and a huge, mirrored bar was on the right. Looking around, he spied a table with two empty chairs. "Looks like we're in luck."

Making their way to the table, he assisted her into a chair and scooted the other one next to her before sliding in. A moment later, a server came by to take their order. He asked for a Guinness, and she ordered a cranberry vodka.

"Other than a glass of wine, I can't tell you the last time I went to a bar and got a drink. Not since… well, not since before Matt died."

He leaned back in his chair, his arm resting on the back of hers with his hand gently massaging the back of her neck. His attention was focused completely on her beauty as it stole his breath, and he wondered if it always would. Their drinks were delivered and he lifted his, waiting to tap against her drink. "I feel like I'm going to repeat everything your father said, but I want to make sure you know how proud and impressed I am with you. Getting your degree with everything you've had to deal with is huge. But you did it, babe." Their glasses clinked and they sipped their drinks before he leaned over to steal another kiss.

"I thought I saw you sitting over here and wanted to come to say hello, but then I hate to interrupt you and your beautiful lady."

Ben looked up and spied Daniel Anderson standing next to a man that was so much like him Ben felt sure it must be a relative. Leaning over, they shook hands. "Daniel, good to see you again." He turned toward Violet, placing his hand on the back of her chair. "This is Violet Mayfield. And this is Daniel Anderson, who owns Anderson Construction."

Daniel and Violet shook hands, and Daniel smiled. "It looks like the two of you are celebrating."

"Yes, we are. She just finished her degree in business management."

"Congratulations," Daniel said. "That's quite an accomplishment." The other man stepped forward, and Daniel continued the introductions. "This is my brother, Dave. He's part-owner of Anderson Construction. Dave, this is another veteran… a former SEAL. He has hands-on experience and is thinking about going into contracting." A new round of shaking hands took place.

Ben nodded. "I'm still working on my grandmother's house, and I'm getting some work done on Violet's. But I'm definitely interested in talking with you. I called the other day and left a note with the receptionist."

"Fuc… fudge," Daniel cursed then covered quickly, his gaze glancing apologetically toward Violet. "I had a receptionist, but I didn't get your message, Ben. But then, I wasn't getting a lot of messages." He chuckled and shook his head. "Not getting messages is one of the reasons I don't have a receptionist anymore."

Dave huffed, shaking his head as he looked at his brother. "I'm more of a silent partner and not there much. What we are in serious need of is an office manager who can run the whole office, but that's not easy to find."

"Why is it not easy?" Violet asked.

Daniel shrugged, rubbing his chin. "We're a small,

family-run business, but we're busy as hell and growing. The problem is that we need someone who can manage an office, handle the ordering, handle some of the crew and work assignments, plus be a receptionist, and can handle basic bookkeeping. We've got an accountant for our taxes, but it's hard to find somebody. Usually, someone either comes with no experience and they can't handle all that, or they're looking to climb the corporate ladder and don't like a job where jeans are as good to wear as fancy clothes."

Ben stared at Violet, seeing the wheels turn behind her eyes. Glancing up at the two Anderson brothers, they were watching her closely as well.

"I don't suppose you're looking for a job, are you?" Daniel chuckled as he moved his gaze between Violet and Ben.

"As a matter of fact, I am. My experience is in book-keeping, and I've certainly worked as a receptionist. And now, I have a degree in business management." Her gaze darted over to Ben, and with his hand on the back of her neck, he could feel both her nerves and excitement.

"Well, we'll let you get back to your celebration, but Ben, send me an email. That way I'll be sure to get it and we can talk about you, your construction goals, and what we can do for each other." He pulled out another business card and slid it across the table toward Violet. "And Ms. Mayfield, if you're interested, you can come by and check us out, and we'll be more than happy to interview you." He turned toward Dave and said, "And just think, I almost didn't come over here and interrupt them." With a laugh and a wave, the two Anderson brothers walked away.

Violet made big eyes at Ben, then leaned forward, touching her forehead to his. "Can you believe that just happened?" she whisper-squealed.

"Pretty amazing, I'd say."

Her brow crinkled, and he lifted his hand to gently smooth the crease. "What sent you from happy to concerned in the span of two seconds?"

"Would it be weird if we ended up working in the same place?"

"Violet... let's not start worrying about *what-ifs* that aren't even here yet. Plus, if I work for them, I'll be out on job sites."

She sucked in her lips between her teeth and nodded. "What do you think about it, though?"

He kissed her lightly. "I say sleep on it, and if you still like the idea tomorrow, then arrange to go by and see what they need. Go slow, make sure you think it's what you want and that you're not just taking a job to get you out of where you are now. Talk to them. Look around. Discuss benefits, salary, duties. And then sleep on it again. If it's still good, then I think you'll know what to do."

She held his gaze, her delicious lips curving until a smile spread across her face. Lifting a brow, she whispered, "Sleep on it, you say? What if there's something else I want to do in bed tonight?"

His brows jumped to his hairline. "Damn, woman." Slapping money on the table to pay for their drinks plus a huge tip, he hopped down, waved toward the server, and turned to lift Violet down from her stool. With his hand wrapped around her waist, they fast-walked out of the bar. As soon as they were outside, he whirled her around, and with both hands cupping her face, he drew her closer. Their lips met and flamed immediately. He kept it short, dragging his mouth from hers, already his breath heaving.

"Home?"

She smiled and nodded. "Yeah, let's go home."

19

As soon as they entered Violet's townhouse, Ben flipped the deadbolt. He turned and hesitated for only a second as they stood, staring at each other. Then, as if on cue, they reached out and grabbed each other's hands and raced toward the stairs. He hadn't felt this primed since he was a teenager, and hoped he had more finesse... but at the rate they were taking the stairs two at a time together, he doubted finesse was on either of their minds.

Reaching the bedroom, he dragged in a breath as his heart pounded, feeling as though he'd just finished a twenty-mile run in full pack.

Violet kicked off her shoes and her fingers went to the side zipper of her dress. Not waiting, he fumbled with the buttons on his shirt, almost popping them off in his haste. Jerking it off at the same time he toed off his shoes, his belt buckle was next. Stripping in record time, they stood in the middle of her bedroom, both naked but several feet apart. His gaze raked over her body, the soft curves and dips begging his hands and lips to explore.

She slowly lifted her hands to her head and deftly removed the clip holding the dark tresses from her face. Now free, the waves fell down her back, over her shoulders, and the ends hung in the front, allowing her nipples to peek through.

His breath caught in his throat, almost afraid to exhale as though the apparition in front of him would disappear. A chuckle erupted from deep inside his chest, and her questioning gaze showed a tinge of insecurity. Rushing to explain, he said, "We've got all night. All night just for us. And yet here we are, in a big hurry as though we're on the clock for the fastest sex in the history of time."

Now it was her time to laugh. He loved the sound coming from her, but his gaze took in the way her hair rippled and her breasts moved with her mirth.

She stepped forward a foot, maintaining a space between them. "As a mom, especially a single mom, it seems as though anything that's just for me has to be done quickly. A bath... a facial... a nap."

He moved another foot forward until their bodies were only an inch apart, and he lifted his hand to cup her face, his thumb sweeping over the petal-soft skin. The rich color of her eyes was not as discernable in the barely-lit room but their intensity still burned straight through him. "We don't have to rush. Not tonight. We have the entire night to do whatever we want. To touch, feel, explore, learn... to make love."

"All night?" Her hopeful whisper escaped as her eyes widened.

"Yeah… all night."

"That sounds like… forever."

Drawing her closer, he bent and took her mouth. This time it was slower, his tongue gliding over her lips and as she sighed. He entered, and his tongue tangled with hers. His cock was already at full mast, but now, pressed against her soft tummy, he had to focus on the kiss to keep from tossing her onto the bed.

His arms slid around her back, offering gentle pressure until her front was plastered to his. Picking her up with ease, he stalked forward until the backs of her legs hit the mattress. Bending with her still in his arms, he grabbed the comforter and jerked it down. Setting her on the side, he continued to kiss her as he bent over her until she was fully lying on the sheets. His hands trailed a path from her shoulder down to her breasts, palming their fullness before tweaking her nipples.

Leaving her delicious mouth, he dragged his lips over the path his fingers had just taken. Nipping and sucking, he grinned at her squirming as he pulled her nipple deeply into his mouth. Her hands first clutched the sheets and then grabbed onto his shoulders as his hand glided over her tummy to press his thumb on her clit.

Her hips undulated upward, and only too glad to acquiesce to her unspoken desires, he kissed his way lower until the scent of her arousal filled his nostrils, and his mouth was busy as he licked her slick folds. Nectar. It was the only word he could think of to describe the unique scent and taste of her. Wanting more, he shouldered her thighs wider and angled his body for the fullest enjoyment as his tongue plunged inside her sex.

Her legs quivered for a moment, and he felt her body tense under his fingertips. Her nails dragged over his scalp and the slight sting urged him on. His mouth moved up as he slid a finger inside her channel, and he sucked her engorged clit. With the house to themselves, her uninhibited cry rocked through him, and he fuckin' loved the sound of his name on her lips.

Her body shook slightly, and he kissed his way back to her lips, keeping his weight off her chest with his forearms planted next to her shoulders and his fingers threading through her hair. A light sheen of perspiration dotted her forehead and a few tendrils of dark hair stuck to the moisture. He gently brushed the hair from her face, not willing to take his eyes off her beauty. His heart pounded just from watching her come apart, and even though his eager cock was ready, he could have laid by her side, just watching her glow.

Neither spoke for a long moment before she lifted her hand and gently ran her fingers over his face. "What are you thinking?"

Her whispered words moved through him and he smiled. "I didn't expect this."

She continued to caress his face, smoothing the tips over his skin and through his hair. The touch was light, feather-soft, and he leaned his head into her palm.

Knowing his words made no sense by themselves, he continued. "This. Us. You."

Her lips pulled in but her eyes appeared to smile.

He chuckled and shook his head, trying to put into words what he felt. "I had no clue what my future held when I left California. Out of the only job I knew. Coming to an unknown situation with my grandmother. A minimum plan of helping her get settled somewhere else would then mean I needed a place to go. For four days, I drove across the country, wondering what the hell I was going to find at the end of the journey."

"And what did you find?"

"I found what I had been missing and didn't even know it." He leaned forward, kissing her lightly. "I found a chance to help the woman who saved me when I was a child. I discovered a kinship with two children who are now in my heart. And I found you... when I least expected my heart to find someone, there you were."

The rasp of her sudden intake of air followed by her top teeth landing on her bottom lip had him lean in and kiss her again. The slow, languid kiss sent sparks throughout his body and his no-longer patient cock ached. Rolling over her, he scooted back onto his heels to grab the condom from the top of her nightstand where he'd tossed it earlier. Sheathed, he kept his upper body high off her chest with only his hands planted next to her and his cock lined up at her entrance.

She dropped her knees to the mattress, exposing her slick beauty to his perusal, and with his tip at her entrance, he thrust deeply. Her legs shot upward, clinging to his waist and her heels digging into his ass.

A groan left his lungs as her heat encompassed him, gripped him, and threatened to take him over the edge too quickly. *Fuck, I'm no teenager!* Determined to not embarrass himself, he turned his focus to where it should have always been... on Violet. The way her dark hair flowed over the pillow. The way her blue-purple eyes stayed pinned on his face, passion clearly visible in their depths. The way she bit her bottom lip as though holding back, trying to stay silent.

Lowering his upper body as he continued to thrust deeply, he kissed her lips, soothing over the abraded flesh with his tongue, eliciting moans from her he wanted to hear. "It's only us, babe. You can let go."

His whispered words had the desired effect as her body began to undulate in time with his, lifting her hips to meet his, forcing his cock deeper, his pelvis dragging against her clit. Her eyes widened and she cried, "Oh, God, that's... that's..."

Not caring that she couldn't find the right word to describe what she was feeling, he grinned. He loved watching as she let loose the passion he knew she had. Passion for her family. Passion for life. And now, passion for him.

He leaned down again and kissed her lips before gliding his mouth over her jaw and neck, nipping at the pulse point that he'd focused on earlier. Watching her pulse increase with his movements had been heady, and now he wanted to feel her lifeblood against his tongue. He was barely aware of the light sting of her fingernails digging in the muscles of his back.

No longer able to ignore his own body's response,

he felt the burn in his lower back and his balls tightening. Wanting her to come again, he dropped even lower and pulled a nipple deep into his mouth, his teeth dragging lightly over the sensitive bud. Her body began to quiver and her legs tightened around his hips as they continued to piston.

Suddenly, her quivering stopped and her entire body tensed. Ben was aware of each sensation—her heels digging into his ass, her thighs squeezing his waist, her arms tightening around his shoulders, her neck arched back pressing her breasts upward, and her eyes shut as she cried out loudly.

Seeing Violet in the throes of an orgasm… fuckin' beautiful. And so fuckin' different. An orgasm for a past lover or one-night stand had been nothing more than the precursor that let him know he could come with the satisfaction that his partner had gotten off as well. But with Violet, her pleasure meant more to him than his own.

No longer holding back, he let himself go, and with every muscle corded with tension and lights prickling the dark behind his eyelids, he roared through his own release. Continuing to thrust into her tight channel, milking every drop from him, he finally fell to the side, his muscles spent. Boneless, with no other thought other than forcing oxygen into his lungs, he clung to her as his body and mind recovered from the most intense orgasm he'd ever experienced. He did not doubt that if Bear Black, his former SEAL team leader, had ordered him to move, he wouldn't be able to comply.

Slowly, consciousness returned, and he was intimately aware of the precious woman in his arms. As their breathing and heartbeats slowed, they lay facing each other as his cock slid from her body, but their legs remained tangled. He didn't want to leave but had no choice. Kissing her lightly, he mumbled, "Be right back." With as much haste as he could manage, he dealt with the condom in the bathroom and washed his hands before rejoining her in bed, wrapping her up and re-tangling their legs just as before.

"About that..." she began, then hesitated, her brow crinkled.

"About what?"

"Um... the condom."

Not sure where she was going with this, he brushed the sweat-damp hair from her face and glided his fingers along her cheek, giving her a chance to pull her thoughts together.

Finally, she held his gaze, and with her usual honesty said, "I know we haven't discussed this, but please, understand... after finding out about my husband's affair, I feel it needs to be said. I was faithful to him and take that commitment seriously. As long as you and I are in a relationship, there will be no one else."

His thumb continued to sweep gently over her cheek, and he nodded. "I know it must be hard for you to trust after what you went through. And I know that any vow I make to you will lose some of its meaning because of what he did. But I make the same promise to you that you just made to me, Violet. As long as we're in a relationship, there will be no one else. I will always be a strong link in the chain that is us and will spend every day proving that to you."

She held his gaze for a long moment, then her lips slowly curved. Her hand lifted and gently soothed over his face. "I believe you."

"Can I ask what you meant when you brought up the condom?"

Licking her lips, a light blush crossed her cheeks. "I know it's the safe thing to do. I'm on birth control, but I realize that women can always say that and a man doesn't know for sure, so a condom is more of a guarantee for him. But, of course, a condom is also a security against STDs. I haven't been with a man since my husband died four years ago. But I did get tested after I found out he'd been unfaithful, and thank God, I'm clean."

"We were tested all the time in the military, and I'm clean as well. Plus, I haven't been with a woman before you in a long time. But I've got no problem getting tested again." Her smile warmed his heart, and he kissed her lightly. "What does all of this lead to?"

"I just thought that if we're clear on our understanding and both clean, then we could forgo the condoms. As long as you trust that I'm on birth control."

"Babe, I completely trust you, but let me just say that if something happened and you got pregnant, I'd be over the fuckin' moon." Her eyes shot open, and he chuckled. "Seriously, Violet. I don't plan on going anywhere. I'm in this for the long haul. You, Lily, Charlie, and anyone else who comes along. I know we're still early days, but that doesn't make what we feel any less real."

Moisture gathered in her eyes, and he swept his thumbs underneath her lashes.

"Could you be any more perfect?" she asked.

"I'm not perfect, sweetheart. But I do think we are perfect together."

Pulling each other closer, he rolled to his back with her plastered on top. She looked down and grinned. "Are you game for another round since we have the house to ourselves?"

His smile matched hers as he jutted his hips upward, his cock already responding to the feel of her body and her words. "Hell, yeah, babe. Bring it on."

She bent forward and kissed him, doing exactly that.

20

Violet walked through the upstairs, gathering clothes from the laundry baskets to take downstairs. The sun flowed through the windows and she felt a lightness in her soul that she hadn't felt in a long time.

In the past week, she had taken Daniel Anderson up on his offer and spent a morning at Anderson Contracting, spending the time obtaining a bird's-eye view on what the company needed and then interviewing for the position of Office Manager/Bookkeeper. The building was large considering most of the space was a warehouse that housed their trucks, tools, and a multitude of building supplies. The office in the front was much smaller, fairly utilitarian and yet comfortable.

During the interview, she had the opportunity to get to know Daniel and Dave a little better. Daniel had been married to his high school sweetheart for over fifteen years and they had three children. He'd been at the helm of the veteran-owned and run business since he got out of the Navy and his father was ready to turn it over.

Dave had been divorced for several years, and while he didn't work daily for the construction company, he kept active in the family business.

She had wondered if Ben would accompany her to the office, but he'd insisted that this was her interview. She loved that he was supportive, would give his opinion if asked, but ultimately left the decision up to her. In truth, the decision was not a difficult one to make. She would be able to organize and run the office the way she saw fit. Working for the Anderson brothers would be far superior to spending more years dodging Fred.

But the most important thing was the sense of family. Daniel's wife worked two mornings a week and his mother still popped in occasionally when she was bored at home. She'd met both women and they were thrilled that Violet would consider the position since neither of them wanted to work full-time and were tired of the inefficient, part-time receptionists that had rotated through the office. When Daniel presented her with the salary, benefits including insurance, vacation days, and the ease of knowing if her children became sick she could get to them, it made her decision easy.

She had turned in her two-week notice to Fred, who had not taken her *rejection* very well. He'd insisted that she could clean out her desk and leave by the end of the week, which had not been a hardship. Yesterday, she'd packed a small box of personal items, hugged her other coworkers goodbye, and almost skipped to her car with a huge smile on her face. When she'd called Daniel, he was thrilled, and she would start with them on Monday.

Now, it was Saturday morning, the kids were in the backyard playing with Colleen, and Tara was coming over for lunch. Loading the washing machine, she peered out into the yard, watching as the three children ran with Bounder in Anna's yard. Ben and Anna had insisted the kids could play in their yard since none of the mysterious sinkholes had appeared on their side of the fence.

A knock on the front door caused her to glance at the clock, surprised the morning had passed so quickly. She welcomed Tara in and ushered her to the kitchen where she was ready to prepare sandwiches. "The kids are still out back. Well, technically in Ben's backyard with his dog."

Tara poured chips into a bowl, sneaking a few for herself. "Oh, Colleen wants a dog. Carter and she are going to go look for one soon. That's their summer project. Get a dog... train a dog... then I'm sure I'll end up feeding and walking *their* dog."

Violet laughed and nodded. "I have to admit that it's great for Ben to have the dog. My kids can enjoy him, but I don't have to take care of him."

"At least not now..."

Turning to stare at her friend, she inclined her head. "Okay, just what does that mean?"

Tara pushed the chips away, mumbling, "I don't need more calories," then dusted her hands off before smiling at Violet. "Well, I get the feeling that Ben is important to you. That doesn't mean that you and he will continue a relationship, but if you do, then that dog out there would become yours."

She held her friend's gaze as her lips curved upward, then glanced down, almost in embarrassment at how wide her smile was.

Tara laughed. "I was getting ready to say that maybe Ben was just your neighbor with benefits, but your face tells a different story."

"You know I wasn't looking for anyone. I had been happy in my marriage, or at least happy in my ignorance." She saw Tara start to speak and rushed, "I know none of what Matt did was my fault. And as strange as it sounds, even knowing what I know, I would've never wished him to have been killed. Eventually, I would've found out about the affair, and he and I would've had to dissolve our marriage while deciding how to handle custody of the children. But once he was gone, I was more than satisfied to stay single and revel in being just a mom to Charlie and Lily."

Tara reached over and placed her hand on Violet's arm, giving a little squeeze. "And then Ben came into the picture."

"Yep, just like in a ridiculous Hallmark movie, I've fallen for the man who moved in next door."

"Hey, don't mock Hallmark movies. Believe me, there were many times when my marriage dissolved that I would watch a chick flick while drinking a glass of wine after Colleen had gone to bed. Like you, I never thought about meeting someone. I certainly never went looking."

"At first, I thought he was just a good neighbor. Helping out his grandmother, not getting upset if my kids peppered him with a thousand questions, adopting a stray dog, and then offering to do some work on my house. Throughout all that, he became someone I enjoyed being with. If he was a friend only, that would be fine." Another wide grin split her face. "Of course, by then, I was secretly in lust with him, but I would've tamped that down so that we could be friends only."

Tara leaned back and with great drama clapped her palm against her heart. "Oh, unrequited lust for a man in the friend zone."

"That sounds ridiculous, doesn't it?"

"No, not really. I think if that's all Ben had wanted, you would've fallen into that role. I'm just glad he saw how wonderful you are and is in a place in his life where he wants that."

The two women were quiet for a moment, then Tara asked, "And how serious are you two?"

"We haven't spoken of love, although we both admitted we are *falling* for each other. That seems so adolescent, but I think we're both almost afraid to mention the word love until we're sure."

"Nope, not adolescent at all. Rushing the feelings or the declarations of love would be adolescent. You're a widow, a mother, and not ready to take another leap unless you're sure. He's been in the military, used to men and missions, and not ready to jump into a permanent relationship unless it's right."

Violet nodded, Tara's words striking to the heart of the matter. "But I will confess I think that's the direction we're heading."

Tara slid from the stool and moved directly into Violet's space, wrapping her arms around her. The two women hugged before the sound of the back door slamming open caused them to look around as the children rushed inside.

"Hey, guys, go wash your hands—"

"Mom!" her kids all shouted at once.

"A creepy man has been sitting across the street staring at us forever!" Lily huffed, a scowl on her face.

"I think he's the bad man," Charlie said, his voice subdued as his gaze darted between his sister and mom.

Without hesitation, Violet rushed past the children and through her back door, looking beyond the side street that bordered her fence at the park. There was no bench nearby, but a man was leaning against a tree, looking down at the phone in his hand. Marching to her gate, she threw it open and moved onto the sidewalk, stopping only at the street to see if it was clear of traffic before crossing.

He looked up, his eyes widened, and he turned and started to run away.

"Hey! You!" Rage filled her body as she ran down the sidewalk, but he'd darted across the busy street that passed in front of her house, and with cars moving up and down the road, she couldn't safely cross. "Dammit!" Realizing she didn't have her phone, she had no way to take his picture or call for help.

Turning, she stomped back toward her backyard, Tara standing near the fence with her phone in her hand. "The kids are inside where it's safe, and I've called Carter."

Her body began to shake with anger, and Tara

wrapped her arms around her. "Thanks, Tara, I'm glad you were here. I need to get to the kids."

Tara held on for another moment, saying, "Give yourself a moment. The kids are fine and they need to see that you are, too."

Knowing her friend was right, she breathed deeply for a moment, trying to still the red-hot anger that flowed like lava through her bloodstream. Swallowing deeply, her head nodded in jerky movements, and the two women went back inside. One look at her children's faces and she dropped to her knees as they rushed to her.

"Mom, don't be mad, but I called Ben," Charlie confessed. "He always said I could call him if I needed to."

"Baby, I'm not mad. Well, not at you." She stood and ushered the kids into the living room, glancing at Tara. Leaning toward her friend, she whispered, "I'll let you handle Colleen any way you want."

"Carter is on his way, and as a detective, he'll want to know what they saw. And I want Colleen here so that she'll know her friends are being taken care of."

Nodding, she let out a shaky breath. Not sure how to prepare the kids for Carter's arrival, she sat on the sofa with them, each on a side with her arms wrapped tightly around them. "Colleen's stepdad is a detective, and he's coming over. He'll want to make sure you're safe, and he'll have some questions for us."

"Just like on TV," Charlie said, his voice much surer now that he was tucked into his mom's embrace.

Before she had a chance to respond, a knock

sounded on her front door at the same time her back door slammed open. She jerked her head from side to side in surprise. Ben raced in from the back as Tara opened the front door, allowing Carter to enter.

Violet stood, but Lily and Charlie were faster, rushing to Ben as he squatted, his arms swooping around them. Her breath caught in her throat and her heart pounded as she witnessed the man she'd fallen in love with tightly holding her children safely in his arms. After a moment, his eyes opened and zeroed in on her. She offered a tremulous smile, not sure she would be able to speak.

Ben stood, keeping his hands on Lily's and Charlie's shoulders, and moved toward her. Her feet became unglued and she rushed to him, the four engulfed in another hug. Turning, she spied Carter standing next to Tara, Colleen in his arms.

"I'm so sorry that something happened while Colleen was here."

Carter waved away her concern and said, "Let's sit down and find out what happened. Once I know that I'll have a better idea of how to proceed."

She had no idea what *proceed* meant to the detective but followed his instructions as she ushered the children to the sofa. Sitting in the middle, she was comforted when Ben sat next to her, Charlie tucked into his side and Lily pressed against hers. Tara sat in the chair with Colleen perched with her, and Carter brought in one of the dining room chairs.

"Okay, kids," Carter began, "can you tell me what you saw and what happened today?"

The three kids looked at each other, and Violet suggested, "Lily, as the oldest, do you want to start?"

Her daughter held her gaze and nodded slowly before gaining an encouraging nod from Ben. Turning toward Carter, she said, "We were just playing in the back. We'd walked over to Ben's yard 'cause it's bigger and the dog is there. Plus it doesn't have any holes."

"Holes?" Carter's gaze darted to Violet.

"I'll fill you in on that," Ben said softly, and Carter nodded, turning his attention back to Lily.

"I can't run with my sprained ankle, so I was sitting on the deck. A noisy motorcycle went down the road next to our house, and I looked over. That's when I saw the man across the street at the park. I didn't think anything about it first. I thought maybe he was waiting on somebody."

"Was he doing anything specific... sitting, standing, talking to someone..." Carter asked.

Lily shook her head. "No, he was just leaning against a tree. Colleen and Charlie were in the yard tossing a ball to Bounder, and sometimes he'd bring it to me and I'd toss it, too. Bounder was excited and raced toward the fence near the sidewalk, and that's what made me look again. The man was still standing there, only this time he had a phone in his hand, and I think he was taking pictures of us."

Violet gasped, and Ben jerked. She was horrified at the thought that someone was taking a picture of her children, but her attention slid to Ben as she felt the tension rolling off of him. As angry as she was, she wanted to make sure he was holding on to his emotions so he wouldn't frighten the kids. She glanced to the side, but other than the tick in his jaw, he looked perfectly calm as he rubbed his hand over Charlie's back.

Focusing on Lily, she forced a smile onto her face and nodded. "You're doing really well, sweetheart."

"Did the man seem to notice you looking at him?" Carter asked.

"If he did, he didn't change what he was doing. He just leaned against the tree and looked down at his phone and then brought it back up again. Maybe he wasn't taking our picture, but I started getting a weird feeling in my stomach."

Charlie piped up, "Lily called us over and we all came up on the deck with Bounder. She whispered to us that she thought someone was across the street but didn't want us to all look at the same time. So we were real sneaky and peeked. She was right. He just kept standing there and stared at us with his phone. I thought he might have been the bad man who dug the holes."

Carter had taken out a pad of paper and was scribbling notes. At Charlie's comment, he looked up but said nothing as Violet offered a slight shake of her head. "Can you describe him for me?"

"I saw him," Violet answered in place of the children. She felt Ben's fingers dig into her shoulder as he startled. She turned and looked at him, seeing his calm façade crack. "The kids came running in and said there was the man across the street, possibly the bad man, and I just raced outside. I saw him leaning against the tree looking down at his phone. I started to run across the street toward him—"

Ben's fingers flexed again as he muttered, "What the hell, Violet?"

"I didn't think, Ben. I just reacted. If there was some-body out there who'd been staring at my children, I wanted to know. I was going to find out what he was doing!"

Ben's jaw ticked again, and she had a feeling they'd have more words about her actions, but she had no plans on apologizing for giving in to her mama bear's instinct to protect her cubs. Turning back to Carter, she said, "He was dressed in brown. Brown pants, a brown jacket. Even a brown fedora on his head, which seemed out of place. He didn't see me at first because he was looking down at his phone, but as soon as I started across the street, he looked up and then took off running. Because there were cars on the street, I couldn't dart across, and he got away before I was able to safely get to the other side. I realized I ran out of the house without my phone, so I couldn't call for help or even take a picture of him."

"Did you get a close look at his face?" Carter asked.

"Not very well. He was Caucasian, I'd say late forties, early fifties. Slight build. Shorter than the two of you," she described, inclining her head toward both Ben and Carter. Sighing heavily, she added, "I realize that's not much to go on."

Carter looked toward Tara and smiled. "Sweetheart, can you take the kids for a little bit, and I'll chat with Ben and Violet?"

Standing, Tara held her hands out, and upon receiving nods from Violet, Charlie and Lily stood, also.

"We were just getting ready for snacks," Violet said. "Tara, if you'd like to take them into the kitchen, Lily can show you where everything else is." By now, the adrenaline rush had left her, and she slumped against Ben, grateful for his embrace as he easily took her weight.

Once Tara and the kids had headed into the kitchen, Carter shifted his chair closer to Ben and Violet. "Okay, you want to explain the *bad man and holes* comments from Charlie?"

21

Ben felt as though he were hanging on by a thread. Flashes of missions with his SEAL team flew through his mind.

The time they were racing toward their helicopter hovering just off the ground in the mountainous region of Afghanistan. He was the next to last one on and turned to see Heartbreaker hit the ground as the sound of gunfire erupted. Leaning out, he grabbed Brian by the arm as the bird took flight, pulling his teammate up.

When a hostage rescue on the west coast of Africa took a nosedive after a poisonous snake bit Mars and they had to ditch the original plan, quickly changing roles, managing to get the hostage and Mars out in one piece.

The time he almost didn't make it out of a Mexican drug cartel's mansion because a child stumbled into the area where Ben was setting explosives. Ben had to get the child to safety at the risk of his own as well as his team's.

There were a hundred other memories… but nothing was like the feeling he had when Charlie's voice on the other end of his phone said, "Ben, can you come home? There's a scary man staring at us, taking pictures."

When the call came in, he was almost home, having spent the afternoon at Anderson Construction with Daniel. On a high, having accepted a job while working on becoming a licensed contractor, he was in a hurry to get home so that he could celebrate with his grandmother, Violet, Lily, and Charlie. But as soon as he heard Charlie's words, he stepped on the accelerator, his heart pounding until he rushed into Violet's house and saw for himself that the kids were safe. Knowing the kids would take their panic cues from him, he called upon his SEAL training and locked down his emotions.

Now, sitting with his arm around Violet and facing Carter, he explained what Charlie saw out his window and how they all initially thought it was nightmares. "To be honest, even Charlie seemed confused as to whether or not he was awake or asleep at first. Then he admitted that he had looked out the window to see a man in the yard."

Carter's brows drew down, but he remained silent, still scribbling in his notebook. As Ben described how Lily's twisted ankle led him to canvas the yard, he explained the lifted sod and soft dirt that had been disturbed.

"What the fuck?" Carter asked, then winced, his gaze shooting toward the kitchen. Turning back to Ben and Violet, he said, "Any idea what's going on?"

"None. I installed motion sensor security lights. He may have come back and discovered the lights. That could be why he's taking pictures and keeping an eye on the yard from across the street."

"I'm going to give this to a detective who works in the precinct in this area. I know there might not be much he can do, but at least I'll pass it on."

Ben held Carter's gaze and nodded. "I don't know what the fuck is going on, but I'm stepping things up." Anger flooded his being, but his training had him already calculating a mission that included his family's safety. *And Violet, Charlie, and Lily are my family.*

"Oh, Ben, do you think the kids are in danger?"

He squeezed Violet's shoulder as he shifted on the sofa, facing her. "Babe, I want you and the kids to move in with me and Babciu. There's plenty of room, and that way I know you'll be safe until we know what's going on. I'll set up security cameras on the outside of your house."

If he expected Violet to argue or disagree, he breathed a sigh of relief when she held his gaze and then nodded slowly. "Okay… yes… whatever we need to do."

"I don't think anyone is after them, but I'm not taking a chance. But we'll get you all settled in Babciu's house, and then I'm going to get started here." He stood as Carter did, and the two men shook hands.

"I promise I'll let you know what the detective says," Carter said, placing his hand on Violet's shoulder. He called for Tara, and she appeared with the children.

Violet and Tara hugged goodbye with promises to

get together soon, and Ben walked the Fiskes to the front door. Charlie and Lily stood to the side, their eyes wide as Ben called them over and squatted to their level again.

"Okay, guys, here's the deal. I want to make sure you and your mom are safe. So, we're going to gather your things and for a while, you three are going to move in with me and Babciu."

"Really?" Charlie asked, his eyes wide. "Can I sleep in her top room, the one that goes out onto the roof deck?"

"Absolutely not," Violet interjected. "The last thing I need is for you to sleepwalk and end up on the roof! We'll sleep wherever Anna allows!"

Ben chuckled as he ruffled Charlie's hair, glad that to a six-year-old, his enthusiasm had great recuperative powers. "I need to go over and let Babciu know what's going on. You two help your mom by listening to her as you pack up what you need."

Lily appeared deep in thought before she asked, "How long will we stay?"

Ben and Violet exchanged a look. "I don't know, honey. But until we know what's going on, we'll all be one big happy family over at Babciu's house, okay?"

At the word *family*, both kids grinned. "I'll go pack! We won't be a trio anymore," Charlie shouted as he ran upstairs. "We'll be a quintet!"

Lily followed her brother with just as much energy, and Ben turned to pull Violet closer. "The kids will be fine. But how about you?"

Her gaze shifted over his shoulder to the now-empty stairs. Heaving a sigh, she said, "Jesus, Ben, earlier…

when I raced outside, if I could have reached that man, I would have pulled him limb from limb."

"I know, sweetheart. I felt the same when I got the call from Charlie. Terrified. Fuckin' terrified. Never felt that sense of helplessness until I got in here and saw that you all were okay."

She nodded slowly. "The kids seem okay. They're obviously thrilled we get to go to your house."

"Speaking of that, let me go talk to Babciu." Seeing Violet open her mouth and knowing she was about to thwart his plans, he rushed, "She'll be thrilled. I promise." Kissing her lightly, he nudged her up the stairs and hustled through the back door, hopping the fence as he ran to explain what was happening to his grandmother.

An hour later, he ushered Violet and the kids through the upstairs. "Okay, Charlie, this is your room. It used to be mine, so I hope you like it."

"Wow, it's bigger than my room at my house," Charlie said, his eyes wide and his smile firmly planted on his face.

"Well, when my grandfather worked to put both houses together, there were six smaller bedrooms up here and he enlarged them when he tore out walls and made four from the six."

Violet entered the room with Charlie and helped him put some clothes into a drawer that Ben had cleared out as well as a few of his toys into the corner. Ben led Lily to the room next to Charlie's. "This one is yours. Babciu loves this room because it gets great morning sunlight."

"Oh, it's pretty," Lily enthused as she looked around

the bedroom decorated with a bright yellow, green, and blue bedspread, pillows, and curtains. Violet popped in to make sure Lily's items were put away as well.

He reached out and snagged her wrist, pulling her to him. Leaning over, he spoke softly. "You okay, babe?"

She nodded, but he could feel her nerves strung tautly. He led her across the hall and they entered the main bedroom. "This was Babciu and Grandpa's room which she no longer uses since she has turned the sitting room downstairs into her bedroom. Honestly, I think she's happier down there anyway. She said this room felt large and empty when she was by herself."

Violet walked over to the low queen-sized bed centered against one wall and turned around. "It's lovely, but it seems much more than I need. Why don't you sleep here?"

"There's another bedroom next to this one. It's fine for me."

"This is so generous for you and Anna to share your home with us—"

"But Mom, Ben said we're one big family. That makes it okay for us to be here." Charlie had popped his head through the door and grinned up at them before running into Lily's room.

Violet rolled her eyes at her son's exuberance, then turned to Ben. "I don't mind telling you that I'm completely overwhelmed right now. I just quit my job, and on Monday start a new one. I just chased a man who I think was taking pictures of my children. And now, I'm out of my house for a bit and living in yours."

He wrapped his arms around her and pulled her close. With one hand on the back of her head, he pressed her cheek against his heartbeat. "I won't let anything happen to you or the kids. I'm going to see to it. Believe me?"

She nodded against his chest. "And us?"

"Together, we're stronger than ever." He kissed the top of her head and squeezed her. "Come on, let's get downstairs. I know Babciu is dying to find out how everyone is doing and wants to make sure you're settled in."

By dinnertime, they were gathered around the table. Babciu's smile was as wide as the children's, and Ben knew she was thrilled to have a house full of people she loved.

"Anna, I can't thank you enough," Violet began. "We'll all pitch in to help with everything, right, kids?"

Charlie agreed immediately, swinging his legs while eating. Lily, on her best behavior with her napkin settled on her lap, beamed toward the others at the table. Charlie finished first and looked around the table, his forehead scrunched.

"What are you thinking so hard about?" Ben asked as the little boy wiped the milk mustache from his upper lip.

"Well, if we're now a quintet but you and Mom have a baby, what will we be?"

The silence only lasted a few seconds but it was deafening.

"A sextet," Lily answered easily, looking down as she pushed the last of her peas around her plate, seemingly unaware of the wide-eyed expressions on the adult faces.

Ben shot a glance toward his grandmother, who was barely able to contain the smile spreading over her face, before looking to the side to see a dropped-jaw, speechless Violet staring at her children.

Before he had a chance to form a response, his babcia stood and reached for the cobbler on the counter. "Quintet, sextet... whatever word you choose, I think family is the nicest," she said, much to the obvious delight of Charlie and Lily as they nodded their enthusiastic agreement.

After dinner and a family movie in the den, everyone seemed exhausted and ready for bed. Ben made sure his grandmother was settled and double-checked the doors and locks before going upstairs. By then, Violet had the kids bathed and in their beds. He stopped by Lily's room and accepted the hug she offered.

"Goodnight, Princess Lily," he said, loving the smile on her face as she squirmed under the covers. He moved to Charlie's room just as Violet was kissing her son goodnight. Charlie looked over his mom's shoulder and called to Ben.

Walking into the room, he bent low over the bed, placing one hand on Violet's back and the other on the covers. "Whatcha need, Charlie-boy?"

"Do you think being here will keep the bad man away?"

He felt Violet's back go ramrod stiff and kept his hand gentle as he smoothed it over her tight muscles.

Patting Charlie's leg with his other hand, he nodded. "You are completely safe here. And tomorrow, I'm going to set up some security cameras, and we'll have a chance to see what's going on."

"Like spy cameras?" Charlie's excitement was barely contained.

Grinning at the boy's ability to change moods so quickly, he nodded. "Yeah, kind of like spy cameras."

The click of toenails on the wooden floor drew their attention to Bounder as he walked into the room. He sniffed Charlie's shoes next to the dresser and then curled up on the rug next to the bed. Charlie grinned and flopped back on the mattress. "With Ben and Bounder... we'll be safe."

With that simple assurance, Violet tucked her son in again and they walked to the door. As Ben flipped off the light, he turned and whispered, "Good dreams, Charlie-boy."

He walked her to the main bedroom and stopped at the door. She looked over her shoulder and tilted her head to the side. "You can come in. After all, it's your house."

"That may be, but for now, this is your space."

She reached out and snagged his hand, pulling him into the room. They walked toward the bed and sat side by side, fingers still linked.

"I realize I'm stating the obvious, but you're exhausted," he said, his thumb gently rubbing over her hand.

Nodding slowly, she agreed. "Yeah, I am."

"Why don't you take a hot bath? You've got a big

bathroom all to yourself and can relax. The kids are fine. We're all safe. And I'll be right across the hall."

"Is this too much for you?" she blurted.

He jerked his head back slightly, not taking his eyes off her. Shifting their positions, he faced her, wanting to hold her gaze. "Too much?"

"This," she exclaimed, her free hand sweeping out toward the room and hallway. "The three of us here, invading your home. The kids talking about a quintet... comparing us to a family."

"What about you? Is it too much for you?"

"I asked you first," she mumbled, then pressed her lips together.

It wasn't enough to quell her smile, and he chuckled. "That sounded like something Lily would say."

Her shoulders shook with her gentle laughter. "You're right." She heaved a sigh. "I'm just afraid that right when you and I were starting to be the *us* you talk about, we suddenly end up living in your house, and... honestly? I don't want it to chase you away."

"Violet, I don't get chased away. I was a SEAL. I ran straight into danger and never thought twice about it. This? This is easy, sweetheart." She continued to stare, and he didn't want to leave anything unsaid that might cause her to worry. "Yes, I want you and the kids safe. Yes, I want to be able to have you close while I figure out who that man was and what he was doing. And no, having you here doesn't feel like too much at all. Quite the contrary. I love having you here."

She licked her lips, a nervous action that caused his mind to shift to her mouth and what he wanted to do with her mouth. Blowing out a breath, he said, "I'd better get out of here and let you get to bed. If I don't leave now, I might not make it to my room."

"That'd be okay with me," she said, leaning closer until their lips were a whisper apart.

Not one to walk away from that offer, he angled his head and sealed their mouths together. Just like always, he felt the jolt throughout his body and his cock responded. She maneuvered around so that she straddled his lap and her hot core nestled directly against his swollen cock.

His tongue swept through her warm mouth, her unique taste like a drug he couldn't get enough of. Sliding his hands to the top of her ass, one hand slipped under her shirt to delight in the feel of her soft skin and the other moved lower to grip her firm ass cheeks. With her breasts crushed against his chest, he fell backward onto the mattress, taking her with him.

For a long moment, they kissed while his hands roamed, and she ground her hips against his. When he was afraid he'd come in his pants, he called upon all his past training to push her back gently, sitting up before assisting her off his lap. Her mewl of discontent was almost his undoing.

With his forehead pressed against hers, he tried to catch his breath and regain his senses. "Damn, babe. You are hard to resist."

She slid from his lap and stood, nodding slowly as one hand lifted to her kiss-swollen lips. "I think maybe I should take that bath you suggested earlier."

He stood and walked to the door before stopping

and looking over his shoulder. "You asked if this was all too much for me." He caught her immediate attention as she held his gaze. Shaking his head slowly, he said, "This is the *us* I've been referring to. You, me, the kids, Babciu. All together. Maybe the circumstances pushed that forward, and there's no doubt we find ourselves in an unusual situation, but we're still heading in the direction I wanted us to go."

She bit her lip as moisture filled her eyes. A small smile escaped, and she said, "It's where I'd like us to go, too." She glanced toward the bed. "I'd ask you to stay, but I'm afraid the kids might need me this first night here."

"We've got all the time in the world, babe," he assured, his heart lighter as she nodded.

Ben had made a late-night call to two of his former SEAL team members, Zig and Bear, just to get their take on the best security camera and system to install. Wanting to know what the hell was going on, he filled them in on the situation. Gaining their expertise, he headed to a local business that specialized in the equipment he needed. Once he made his extensive purchases, he headed home and got to work.

He had installed a camera on the back of his house so it faced the back of Violet's property as well as an angle of the street and park. He installed one on the back of Violet's house also, wanting the most angles he could obtain. The cameras were accessible by his phone and computer. He added a camera to her living room and kitchen. By early afternoon, he was finishing with the installment of a silent alarm for her downstairs doors that would send a signal to his cell phone.

"Ben?"

He turned at the sound of Violet stepping into her

kitchen, followed by Carter and another man. He climbed down from the stepladder and walked over. Placing a hand on her waist, he leaned in for a quick kiss. "Kids okay?"

She smiled and nodded. "Yeah, they're having afternoon movie time since they helped Babciu during the morning." She looked behind her and waved the two men in. "Carter called and said that he had some information for us."

Ben shook hands with Carter, then looked at the other man. Middle-aged, military haircut, dark grey suit. He shook hands as Carter made the introductions.

"Ben, I'd like you to meet Detective Steven Ashburn. Steven, this is Ben Popovich and the homeowner, Violet Mayfield."

"Should we sit down?" Violet asked.

Without waiting for their answer, Ben linked hands with her and said, "I think that's a good idea." He wanted her as comfortable as possible for whatever news the two detectives were bringing. He led them to Violet's living room, glad the kids were not present. Sitting on the sofa, he gently pulled Violet down next to him and wrapped his arm around her. Carter brought the same dining room chair he'd used the day before and Steven took the other armchair.

Once everyone was settled, Carter spoke first. "This isn't my precinct, and as a narcotics detective, it wasn't my area. But I knew Steven from years ago, and I thought he'd be a good place to start. Turns out, he was very interested when I gave him the address."

Steven shook his head as though in disbelief. "I'll be

honest, Ms. Mayfield, when Carter first told me what happened yesterday, I hated that your children were scared but there was little I could do since no crime had been committed. But then he handed me a copy of his notes, and I saw your address."

Inclining her head to the side, Violet said, "I'm sorry, but I don't understand. What about my address struck you?"

"Over a year ago, there was a robbery at one of the branches of the Hope City National Bank. A man named Robert Blaine had worked there for years as a teller. He was close to forty years old at the time, and from all accounts, was well-liked by his coworkers. The day of the robbery, a man wearing a hat pulled low on his head and gloves walked into the bank and made his way to Robert's window. He passed a note to Robert demanding money. Robert was handling it according to the bank's protocol, but when another customer realized what was happening, she screamed, and the perpetrator pulled out a gun. At that point, the situation became dangerous, and he had everyone get on the floor except for Robert, who was to continue putting money into a bag. He raced out of the bank, and it wasn't difficult for the detectives working the case to discover who the thief was. I wasn't the lead detective, but I worked on the periphery of the case so I knew the particulars. Tommy Mancini was arrested, but immediately began saying that he was not the only one involved and claimed he had inside help."

Ben's arm was still around Violet's shoulders, but he glanced down at her hand resting on his leg as her fingers dug into his thigh. "Relax, sweetheart," he murmured, glad when she sucked in a deep breath and let it out slowly.

Nodding toward the detectives, she said, "Please, go on."

"We studied the tapes inside the bank, and then looked at social media, phone calls, anything we could find with the people in the bank and Tommy. It became evident very quickly that Tommy and Robert had known each other in the past. They'd graduated from the same high school even though it appeared they didn't run in the same circles. What we did find is that they had made contact by phone, and using credit card records, we found they'd had lunch together several times. When pressed about Robert, Tommy admitted that Robert had planned everything."

"When Robert was questioned and faced with the evidence that he knew and had met with Tommy before the robbery, he confessed to not planning but assisting out of fear only. Robert made a more convincing case to the judge."

"And the money?" Violet asked.

Shaking his head, Stephen said, "The money was never found. Tommy was convicted on multiple accounts and is still serving his sentence. Robert pleaded guilty to aiding and abetting. He landed an easy sentence, and with good behavior, recently was released on parole."

"My grandmother mentioned this to me, but I forgot

all about it," Ben said, turning to Violet. "Fuck, babe, I'm sorry."

"I still don't understand," she said. "What does this have to do with me?"

"Ma'am, the previous owner of this house had rented it to Robert Blaine. It's my understanding that it sat empty for a couple of months after he was arrested and then you bought it. We are concerned that Robert Blaine may be the person who's come into your yard and was across the street taking pictures. Would you recognize him if I showed you a photograph?"

"I... I don't know," she said but quickly leaned forward to look at the photograph he pulled from his pocket. The man staring back at her was completely ordinary. No identifying marks on his face. Brown hair that was neither long nor short. The photograph must've come before he was incarcerated because he was wearing a white shirt and dark tie. She looked toward Ben and shook her head. "It could have been him, but I have no way of being sure."

"That's okay, Ms. Mayfield," Steven said. "It was a long shot anyway. We have no way of knowing if it was him or not. He is allowed to work and only has to check in with his probation officer. He is not restricted other than to not step into a Hope City National Bank."

"What the hell would he be doing in the backyard?" Ben asked, now furious that this felon might have been around the children.

"Looking for the stolen money," Carter responded. "At least, that would be my guess."

"Why all the holes? If he had it and left it here, wouldn't he know where he hid it?"

"My guess is that Tommy had it all along and had someone hide it. The two have been in contact while in prison. They were in separate facilities but were allowed to use email. It's not private, of course, but since the money was never found, their infrequent correspondence has been scrutinized. It usually seemed to come from Tommy, and Robert would just reply with an insult."

"Anything pertinent?" Violet asked.

"He liked to taunt Robert by sending him quotes. Even from Shakespeare."

Ben jerked his head back, feeling Violet startle as well. "Shakespeare?"

"A victory is twice itself when the achiever brings home full numbers."

Violet stared at Stephen, then shifted her gaze to Carter before twisting around to look at Ben. "That's from Much Ado About Nothing." Her brow crinkled, and she shook her head. "Was that some kind of clue about it being at Robert's home?"

"Ms. Mayfield, to be honest, we had no idea. Until I saw Carter's notes, I never associated that message with anything other than Tommy being a wise guy. Tommy considered himself to be quite the intellectual even though he was a petty thief until the bank robbery, which led him to believe he was more important than Robert. He spent his days leading up to his trial always acting like he was a real know-it-all. Most of the time, we thought he was just a small guy with a big head."

"Was there anything else between the two of them?" Ben asked.

"Several weeks later, another quote from Shakespeare. *Fire that's closest kept, burns most of all.*"

Violet leaned back against the sofa cushions, and Ben took her weight easily. Her fingers were still on his thigh but not as tense as earlier. Shaking her head slowly, she muttered, "I don't recognize that one."

"According to one of the detectives who looked at it, it just comes from The Plays and Poems of William Shakespeare. And before you ask, no, we have no idea if it means anything."

She turned to Ben and shook her head. "Fire that's closest kept? There's no fire here. No fireplace. Not a furnace. Not an outside firepit. Maybe that's why the man stopped coming into the yard. That clue led him somewhere else?"

"If so, then why was the man taking pictures?" As soon as the words left his mouth, he hated the fallen expression on her face. Squeezing her hands, he turned back to the detectives. "Anything else?"

"The last time he sent an email, Robert finally replied and asked Tommy what he was talking about. The response back was another quote. *False face must hide what the false heart doth know.*"

"Detective Ashburn, we appreciate you giving us this information, but I'm not sure what we're supposed to do with it. I've moved Violet and her children into the townhouse directly behind this one where my grandmother lives. I've set up security cameras on the back that would allow me to see if

someone comes in. Starting tonight, I'll turn off the
motion sensor security lights and use my cameras that
can record in the dark to see if someone is around.
I've also installed security cameras in this room and
the kitchen in case someone gets in. All that is wired
to my phone and my computer. I have no idea if the
person who's been coming onto this property is the
same person who was across the street taking cell
phone pictures of the kids. But I know there's little
you can do right now. I just want you to know what
I've set up."

Carter jumped in. "Ben, I get it. You're pissed that
your loved ones are being threatened, but you're a
regular citizen right now, no longer a SEAL. If you see
something, call 9-1-1. Don't be a hero and break the
law."

Ben shoved down the irritation at Carter reminding
him what had been in the past. As any of his teammates
would agree, once a SEAL, always a SEAL. Instead, he
focused on Carter referring to Violet, Charlie, and Lily
as his loved ones. He knew that, he just hadn't said it
yet. *That's gonna change.* Sucking in a deep breath, he
said, "Don't plan on doing anything illegal. But the
HCPD can't do jack-shit right now, so I'm going to. I see
someone in her yard or trying to get into her house, I'll
call for backup and then I'm going in. As you say... I'll
protect my loved ones."

He felt Violet's body jerk and tighten for a few
seconds then relax as she exhaled slowly.

Steven stood and reached inside his jacket pocket,
retrieving a business card. Scribbling on the back, he

said, "Here's my cell. Besides 9-1-1, give me a call if you see anything suspicious."

The others stood as well and shook hands. Violet escorted the detectives to the door and then turned slowly to face Ben after they left. He didn't like the way she held back, not approaching as she kept her gaze pinned to him, an unreadable expression on her face. He knew it was a lot to take in. Overwhelming. Frightening. Maybe she was retreating. Not willing to guess what she was thinking or needing, he stepped forward. "Babe?"

She sucked in a raspy breath then let it out with a ragged whoosh. "You love us."

He stopped advancing, his body lurching slightly as his feet halted in surprise. "What are you thinking, Violet?"

Swallowing audibly, she lifted her hand and dragged her fingers through her thick hair before letting it drop over her shoulder. "A bank robber lived in this house. He walked the same halls my children play in. I mean, you never really think about who owned a house before you... especially since a hundred-and-fifty-year-old house would have had a lot of residents. Maybe there were some really awful people living here before him..."

"Sweetheart..." he said softly, feeling her anxiety ratcheting upward.

"But he was here. Just over a year ago. And now, he's out of prison. And hanging around. Digging holes in my yard." Her gaze shot to the side for a few seconds before slamming back into him and her voice lifted to an almost screech. "Scaring my SON!"

"Babe," he repeated, moving closer. He wanted to envelop her into his embrace but stopped as her palm lifted between them.

"And now, he may have been taking pictures of them? Oh, my God, Ben, I don't know what to do with all of that."

He opened his mouth to speak, but she continued. "And despite all that craziness, all I could think about was that you love us."

Her palm dropped as her chin quivered. He pulled her forward, erasing the space between them, holding her shaky body close to his so that his warmth could surround her. Whispering into her ear, he said, "I do. I've known it but hadn't really acknowledged it, not to myself, not to you. But, yeah, I'm in love with you. You. Charlie. Lily. I had no idea that *forever* was living right behind me."

She leaned back and held his gaze through watery eyes. "I wasn't looking. Not for quick. Not for forever. But I think I began to fall when I saw how wonderful you were with the children. I was terrified for them to fall for you after learning that life can take away so much. I knew they wanted a forever dad but never thought it was living right behind us."

Closing his eyes, he reveled in the feel of her in his arms. The words she whispered against his chest. Her heartbeat pounding next to his. And the love that coursed through his being.

23

Ben awoke, instantly aware of the warm body curled next to his. Violet pressed in tightly, her leg tucked between his and her breath puffing over his chest. He blinked, listening carefully, every SEAL cell tuned in to what had woken him. No sounds were coming from the hall, but he slid from Violet's embrace slowly, ensuring she remained asleep. Picking up his phone from the nightstand, he checked the cameras and saw nothing suspicious. He padded on bare feet into the hall, checking on Lily and then Charlie, finding both sound asleep.

The past week had proven that settling into his babcia's house had not been difficult. His grandmother loved the company and seemed to feel healthier and move better with the others around. The kids were loving the attention and had no problem helping her around the house.

After the revelations from the previous weekend, he

and Violet had sat down with Charlie and Lily to explain that they were *dating*, having decided that word would slowly initiate the kids to the idea of them being together. Violet had assured them that she didn't want them to feel left out as she and Ben became closer.

Lily had grinned widely, barely containing her fist pump, then rolled her eyes and declared, "Geez, Mom. It's okay to kiss him in front of us!"

"Are you gonna share a bedroom like moms and dads?" Charlie had asked.

This question caused Ben's heart to pound as he'd looked toward a wide-eyed Violet, who'd opened and closed her mouth several times before finally muttering, "Uh… well, Charlie…. uh…"

The little boy had continued to swing his legs, a hopeful gleam in his eye. "'Cause I thought we could use that other room as a guest room if Grandma and Grandpa want to come to visit. Or maybe it could be a cool game room."

Ben had slumped back, noting Violet's posture mirrored his. While they had not greatly increased their PDAs nor had they overtly moved into the same bedroom, they had relaxed, knowing the kids were on board.

Since then, he would slip into the main bedroom after the others were asleep, and he and Violet made love as quietly as they could, sparking more desire than he ever thought possible.

Now, he headed downstairs to check on his babcia, finding her asleep as well. Bounder whimpered lightly, and he discovered the dog lying flat, his nose pointed directly to the sliding glass door. With the security light turned off, he could not see beyond the deck. "Something out there, boy?"

His phone vibrated an alert. Picking it up, he checked, seeing the alarm on the front door of Violet's house had been activated. *Fucker used the front door, right on the street!* Since his security lights and the dog had alerted them in the past to the backyard intruder, it seemed whoever was determined to get to something on Violet's property was now staying out of their view by breaking in through the front.

Pulling up the camera feed on his laptop, he watched as a man moved through Violet's living room and dining room and into the kitchen. His heart kicked up a beat as his fingers curled into fists. *If I hadn't moved Violet and the kids into this house they would have been upstairs while that fucker was just below them!*

While watching, Ben looked to his phone where he'd stored Steven's number. With a few punches of keys, he connected. "Steven? It's Ben Popovich. There's a man in Violet's house. I've got him on camera. He's heading to the kitchen."

"Fucking hell. All right, I'm on my way. I should be there in about fifteen minutes, but I'm calling in a unit. They'll come in quietly. You stay put... keep monitoring on the camera."

Disconnecting, Ben watched for a moment, the man's movements inexplicable as he walked directly to the oven. He pulled on first one side and then another, scooting the oven forward, inch by inch. He kept halting the progress, twisting his head as though listening. *He thinks they're upstairs asleep. The fucker went in thinking they were there!*

Rage colored Ben's world red and he slid his feet into shoes by the back door before racing into the basement, past the boxes and old items that needed to be discarded, coming to the door that led to the outside stairs that would keep his presence hidden.

He slipped along the side of the house and down the sidewalk to the back of Violet's house, easily clearing the fence near her trash cans. Crouching in the deep shadows, he watched the screen on his phone again.

The man inside continued to work on the oven until it was pulled out enough that he could slip behind the appliance. He unplugged it from the wall and pulled something from his pocket.

It was difficult to see from the angle of his camera, but Ben watched as it appeared the man unscrewed something from the wall. Ben remembered when his grandfather worked on their kitchen renovation. Most of the old townhouses had at least one fireplace, often more than one. It was either in the living room or the kitchen, being where the family would cook when the houses were built in the mid-to-late 1800s. Many renovations had covered up the outdated fireplaces, but his grandfather loved the look of the exposed brick. He had enclosed the open portion at the bottom, but the brick chimney going up the wall was behind the oven. It was so much a part of the room's décor, Ben never thought about it being a fireplace anymore.

Glancing back to the phone screen showing the camera angle in Violet's kitchen where the man was working, it dawned on him... *Violet's kitchen fireplace had been completely covered, but if someone knew it was there and had access to getting into the panel, they could easily hide something inside.* He dialed Steven again.

"I'm on my way, Popovich!"

"There's a hidden access panel in the old kitchen fireplace that's been covered up during past renovations," he whispered. "I'm watching. The fucker has pulled out something from inside and has walked to the back door."

"I've got a unit almost there," Steven reported. "They're approaching the front."

"Tell them to get to the back, but not to shoot. I'm there now."

"Popovi—"

He disconnected and crouched low just as the man exited Violet's back door, the bag in his hand. The man would have no way out of the yard but to walk right past Ben hiding in the shadows. Legs coiled like springs, Ben was ready. This would be fuckin' easy, but he had to tamp down his anger. If there was one thing he'd learned as a SEAL, keeping calm was essential even on the simplest mission.

Breathing in total silence, he lifted his hands, ready as soon as the man came closer. Suddenly, a blinding light shone in the darkness, and Ben's gaze shot to the back of his house where the kitchen light had turned on. There, standing at the sliding door in plain sight, was Violet, her face close to the glass as she peered out, her hand resting on Bounder's head as the large dog stood peering out as well.

Seeing her there and exposed kicked his steady heartbeat into a wild, erratic staccato. A movement to his side jolted him from his stance as the man still in the dark faced Violet, then turned to run toward Ben.

Launching forward, Ben tackled the man, rolling as their bodies hit the ground until the man ended up underneath him. The satchel flew from the man's hand, bouncing over the grass, but it went unheeded by Ben, whose pent-up anger soared as he held the man to the ground. "Come on, fucker. Fight me." He battled the desire to pound his fist into the man's face, but the man underneath him was thin and shaking, not resisting at all.

The sound of running footsteps sounded in his ears and he looked up to see Steven flanked by a group of policemen rounding the back corner of Violet's house. "Here! I've got him!" Looking toward the image of Violet still standing in the doorway, he shouted, "Turn on the security lights!"

Suddenly, the area was flooded with bright lights, illuminating every corner of the yards. As the police approached with weapons drawn, he called out to Steven, "I've got him on camera getting something from behind the stove in the old, covered-up fireplace. It's over there."

The police hauled the man to his feet, and with the lights blasting down on them, it was easy to see he was Robert Blaine.

Ben leaned forward until he was nose-to-nose with Robert, his fury with this man still overwhelming. "I want to know why you were taking pictures of my kids."

Steven stepped closer to Ben, placing his hand on his shoulder. "Steady," he said before turning to Robert, reading him his rights.

"I don't give a fuck about his rights," Ben growled. "I want to know about the pictures with my kids!"

Robert's eyes widened. "No, no. I would never hurt children. I just wanted pictures of the house I used to live in. I knew whatever Tommy did with the money, he was trying to be such a wiseass. Always thought he was so smart when he was just a stupid man. And he kept taunting me over and over. I just knew he'd hidden the money at my house."

Steven ordered. "Take him in, book him."

Robert jerked his head toward Ben. "No, let me tell him. I would never hurt children. I would never hurt anyone."

"So, why dig holes in the yard?" Steven asked.

"When I got the first message, taunting me about home, I knew it had to be mine. Tommy never stayed in a place long enough to call it home. But he didn't have a key. I came by one day after I got out, seeing there was a family that lived here. There was nowhere in the house for Tommy to have hidden it, so I didn't need to try to disturb anyone. It would just be like him to dig a hole and bury it." Robert shook his head and snorted. "He was so stupid."

"So, you lifted the sod in sections and jammed something in the ground trying to search?" Ben asked. Receiving a nod, he continued, "You made holes all through the yard where children were playing. It never dawned on you that someone could get hurt?"

Robert shook his head, a hound-dog expression on his face. "No, I never thought about that. I didn't want to hurt anyone." He jerked his gaze from Ben's over to Steven's. "I never wanted to hurt anyone. I just wanted what was mine."

"Yours?" Ben jerked his head back. "You helped rob a bank. The place you worked. That money was never yours."

"They owed me! All those years. Never a promotion. Just day after day with the money flowing through my hands. Tommy said it would be easy, but he had no idea how to plan anything. But then he hid it before telling me where and then got caught. All that trouble. All that time. And I had nothing. It was mine!"

"So he kept sending taunting messages."

Robert's face fell again, and he nodded slowly. "Fire… there was no fireplace. And then with the false face message, I remembered when I had the stove worked on years ago, a repairman talked about a fireplace in the kitchen that had been covered up like so many in these old houses. Tommy must have gotten into my house the day of the robbery, stuffed the money there, and then he figured it was safe."

"And then he got caught and you had nothing."

Shoulders slumped, all the adrenaline seemed to have fled Robert, and Steven told the officers to take him to the precinct. Turning to Ben, Steven said, "I'll get your statement tomorrow... well, later this morning since it's already tomorrow."

Nodding, Ben stood in the yard, fists on his hips, staring at the man being led away. Steven looked over his shoulder and chuckled. "And Ben? Thanks for not going total SEAL on him. At least we've got him in one piece."

Ben lifted his chin in response but knew if a man could be arrested for his thoughts, he would be in cuffs for attempted murder. The back of his neck prickled, and he turned to see Violet, now covered in a robe with slippers on her feet, walking toward him, stopping at the fence. He vaulted over the chain-link, wanting... no, *needing* to be close. He let out a long sigh as she slid her hand around his waist.

Looking down, he saw the conflict in her eyes. "You hear?"

Nodding, she sucked in her lips for a moment. "Yeah."

"You okay?"

"No, not really." She peered up into his face, her anguish evident in her eyes and the tension radiating off her body. "He was in my house. What if we'd been there?"

That thought had brought fire to his gut since he'd first seen Robert on the camera in her house. The shakiness in her voice brought his mind back to her, and he wrapped his arms tighter, bringing her to his front where he held her steady. Forcing his words to calm, he said, "He didn't have a weapon. My guess is he would have run off." He had no idea if Robert would have done so or become so desperate that he would have tried to silence them but didn't want Violet to think about that.

"Okay," she nodded against his chest. After a moment, she mumbled, "At least he's caught."

"He won't be back, babe."

Her head nodded in jerks. "And he wasn't after the kids."

"No, he wasn't. He just wanted the money he thought he deserved."

They clung to each other for another moment before she peered up at him again. "You called them *your* kids."

He had but didn't know how she felt about it. The claiming word had slipped out when talking to Robert. He hadn't given it forethought, but at that moment he was raging about someone threatening *his* family. Staring down into her eyes, he couldn't read her emotions but figured it was time to lay it out for her. "In my heart, they are my kids, just like you're mine."

"The *us* you talk about."

Nodding, he breathed a sigh of relief that she seemed to understand. "Yeah... the *us* that's not just here and now but forever."

Her face crumpled as tears slid from her eyes and her arms tightened about his waist. Resting his chin on her head, he held her close as comfort and love swirled around them.

Suddenly, she startled. "Shit!"

His gaze followed her line of sight, and he saw his grandmother standing at the sliding glass door and

Charlie and Lily standing next to her, their faces white and eyes wide. He immediately moved her to his side, still tucked next to him, and started forward toward them. *Time to make sure the whole family knew they were all together... and safe.*

24

THREE MONTHS LATER

Ben drove down the residential street in the north of Hope City, the houses as well as their residents now becoming more familiar. Trees lined the sidewalks in front of the homes and neatly mowed lawns and flower gardens filled the yards. Passing the Fiske house, he waved to Carter as he watered his grass, Colleen prancing in the water, laughing as she was sprayed.

Turning onto another street, he pulled into the driveway of a two-story, red brick house set back from the road. Tall oak and maple trees dotted the front yard, each encircled with a ring of flowers at the base. Flowering shrubs bordered the front porch and side of the house. The driveway led to a three-car garage, enough for their two vehicles and room for a workshop for him.

Parking in the garage, he alighted from his SUV and walked through the door that led to the backyard, following the sounds of children's laughter. A huge swing set, slide, rope climb, and playhouse combination sat to one side under the shade of another large tree.

Charlie was climbing up the rope ladder toward the playhouse fort while Lily pushed on a swing, leaning her head back in laughter.

They were having a blast. Healthy, happy, smiling. And their laughter sparked something deep inside every time he heard it. Reveling in the comfort of knowing they were cared for and loved, they had no lingering effects from the night Robert Blaine had broken into their home.

As soon as he and Violet had entered the house that night, they'd swooped the scared children into their arms and held them close. Babciu had been wrapped into their embrace as well. The noises from the yard and the illumination from the outside lights had penetrated Charlie's and Lily's bedrooms, waking them both. They'd run downstairs, finding his grandmother coming out of her bedroom as well. They'd watched as the police moved around Ben and their mom and placed handcuffs on a man standing between two officers.

Ben immediately ushered them all into the den, settling the whole family around closely. He explained what had happened, who Robert was, and what he had been doing.

Not surprisingly, Charlie had shouted, "I did see a bad man!"

He and Violet let the kids ask questions and answered them as truthfully as they could. Throughout it all, his babcia shook her head and finally praised God that the Mayfields were safely at her house during it all. Ben had to agree with his grandmother's assessment.

She had made hot chocolate, and knowing it would be hard for the kids to go to sleep, he and Violet let them camp out in the main bedroom with them. He'd woken the next morning hanging onto the edge of the bed with Charlie pressed up to him, Lily on the other side of her brother, and Violet hanging off the other edge. He'd smiled… and had never woken up happier.

Violet started with Anderson Construction and in no time at all discovered she loved her new job. Daniel Anderson was easy to work with, she had the autonomy to handle the management of the office the way she saw fit, and she finally felt as though she were using her talents and skills. It was a month before Ben finished with the jobs on the two houses and then he started with Anderson Construction as well.

She and the kids never moved back into their house. At first, they wanted the kids to feel completely at ease and unafraid, but soon, it became apparent that they were happy at Babciu's with their mom and Ben together.

One night, when Violet was out picking up the kids from a playdate, Ben sat down with his grandmother. Asking if she still wanted to sell to move to an independent villa, she'd admitted that she now hated the idea of not being around everyone, but she didn't want to be a burden to him. They'd hugged as he'd assured her that he had no desire to live apart from her.

"You know, Benjamin," she'd said with a smile. "Now that this place is fixed up for a sale, we could stick to that plan. Sell it and find a nice house in the suburbs where the kids can have a big yard to play in."

At first, he'd been stunned by her offer, but she'd patted his leg and said, "After all, a home is anywhere you share it with loved ones."

That very night while they were in bed, he'd talked to Violet about the idea of selling both townhouses and buying a family home. She'd greeted the news with a kiss and then flipped him to his back and shown her enthusiastic agreement by riding him to an orgasm that made him swear the stars glowed brighter over their house.

It only took a few weeks to find a house that they all loved, and with sellers that were relocating, they were ready for a quick sale. Luck stayed on their side with both townhouses selling within two weeks of each other. Packing, moving, and settling had filled their lives until they finally felt like the new house was their home.

Babciu had a downstairs bedroom with her own full attached bathroom. The upstairs had four more bedrooms, much like her old home, but there were two hall bathrooms besides the one connected to the main bedroom that Ben shared with his bride.

They'd married two weeks earlier in a small ceremony attended by family and friends. As he'd stood at the end of the aisle of the little church with Zig and Heartbreaker standing up for him and a few more of his former teammates in the pews with their women, he'd watched as Charlie and Lily walked down the aisle flanking Violet. He'd said he was marrying her but taking them all on as a family.

A weekend trip to an exclusive hotel on the Inner

Harbor of Hope City had been the perfect honeymoon. Neither had wanted to be away from the kids for very long, but a full weekend not leaving their room had been the perfect way for them to start married life.

And now, he stood in the backyard watching Bounder race around as Lily and Charlie played. Looking behind him, he stared through the kitchen window at his grandmother and Violet, smiles on their faces as they worked side by side.

He twisted around as Charlie spied him and raced over, followed by Lily. His arms wrapped around them, greeting them with equal enthusiasm. Violet came to the door and called them in for dinner, a twinkle in her blue-purple eyes as she grinned at him. He turned to jog up the deck steps when one of the neighborhood kids called over the fence.

"Hey, Charlie... can you come over and play later?"

Shaking his head, Charlie called out, "Nah, my dad's home. I'm going to play with him." Waving goodbye, Charlie raced into the house while Ben's feet stuttered to a halt. His chest depressed as air rushed from his lungs, and he blinked the moisture back from his eyes.

Violet let the kids into the house then stepped over, wrapping her arms around him, pulling him in close. "I heard," she whispered.

He nodded, not trusting his voice.

"Are you okay?"

He nodded again. Finally, he looked down at her, seeing tears in her eyes, and said, "I never believed in forever. Now, all I want is to be your forever husband and their forever dad."

Her lips curved into a wide smile, and she lifted on her toes to place a sweet kiss on his lips. "I like the sound of that."

Walking into the house arm in arm, he agreed. "I do, too, babe. I do, too. Forever."

For the next SEALs in Paradise - Holiday Edition
Hot SEAL, Independence Day by Elle James

For all the SEALs in Paradise - Holiday Editions
Hot SEAL, Heartbreaker by Cat Johnson
Hot SEAL, Charmed by Parker Kincaid
Hot SEAL, April Fool's by Becca Jameson
Hot SEAL, In His Memory by Delilah Devlin
Hot SEAL, A Forever Dad by Maryann Jordan
Hot SEAL, Independence Day by Elle James
Hot SEAL, Sweet & Spice by Cynthia D'Alba
Hot SEAL, Labor Day by Cynthia D'Alba
Hot SEAL, Midnight Magic by Teresa Reasor
Hot SEAL, Sinful Harvest by Parker Kincaid
Hot SEAL, Silent Knight by Kris Michaels

Check out Hope City (a series by Maryann Jordan and Kris Michaels)
Hope City Series by Kris Michaels and Maryann Jordan
Brock book 1
Sean book 2
Carter book 3
Brody book 4

Kyle book 5
Ryker book 6
Rory book 7
Killian book 8
Torin book 9

Cael

Jaxon

Jayden

Asher

Zeke

Cas

Lighthouse Security Investigations

Mace

Rank

Walker

Drew

Blake

Tate

Levi

Clay

Cobb

Hope City (romantic suspense series co-developed

with Kris Michaels

Brock book 1

Sean book 2

Carter book 3

Brody book 4

Kyle book 5

Ryker book 6

Rory book 7

Killian book 8

Torin book 9

Saints Protection & Investigations

(an elite group, assigned to the cases no one else wants…or can solve)

Serial Love

Healing Love

Revealing Love

Seeing Love

Honor Love

Sacrifice Love

Protecting Love

Remember Love

Discover Love

Surviving Love

Celebrating Love

Follow the exciting spin-off series:

Alvarez Security (military romantic suspense)

Gabe

Tony

Vinny

Jobe

SEALs

Thin Ice (Sleeper SEAL)

SEAL Together (Silver SEAL)

Undercover Groom (Hot SEAL)

Also for a Hope City Crossover Novel / Hot SEAL...

A Forever Dad by Maryann Jordan

Letters From Home (military romance)

Class of Love

Freedom of Love

Bond of Love

The Love's Series (detectives)

Love's Taming

Love's Tempting

Love's Trusting

The Fairfield Series (small town detectives)

Emma's Home

Laurie's Time

Carol's Image

Fireworks Over Fairfield

Please take the time to leave a review of this book. Feel free to contact me, especially if you enjoyed my book. I love to hear from readers!

Facebook

Email

Website

ABOUT THE AUTHOR

I am an avid reader of romance novels, often joking that I cut my teeth on the historical romances. I have been reading and reviewing for years. In 2013, I finally gave into the characters in my head, screaming for their story to be told. From these musings, my first novel, Emma's Home, The Fairfield Series was born.

I was a high school counselor having worked in education for thirty years. I live in Virginia, having also lived in four states and two foreign countries. I have been married to a wonderfully patient man for thirty-five years. When writing, my dog or one of my four cats can generally be found in the same room if not on my lap.

Please take the time to leave a review of this book. Feel free to contact me, especially if you enjoyed my book. I love to hear from readers!

Facebook
Email
Website